The Plum Tree

The Plum Tree
And Other Short Prose

John Gwilym Jones

Translated by Meic Stephens

With an Afterword by Gwyn Thomas

seren

Seren is the book imprint of
Poetry Wales Press Ltd
Nolton Street, Bridgend, CF31 3BN, Wales
www.seren-books.com

ISBN 1-85411-353-4

A CIP record for this title is available from
the British Library.

The publisher works with the financial assistance of the
Welsh Books Council.

Printed in Plantin by Bell & Bain, Glasgow.

Contents

The Craft of the Short Story

This interview with John Gwilym Jones was conducted by Saunders Lewis and broadcast by the BBC in 1948, shortly after the publication of *Y Goeden Eirin*. It subsequently appeared in *Crefft y Stori Fer* (Y Clwb Llyfrau Cymreig, 1949), together with transcripts of interviews with Kate Roberts, D.J. Williams, J.O. Williams and Islwyn Williams.[1]

This evening we are bringing to a close a series of talks with Welsh short-story writers and, in so doing, we hope to open a door to the future. The four authors who have already taken part had at least two things in common: the work of all four describes a particular district of Wales and the kind of people and way of life that belong to it – the quarry districts, the old characters of Carmarthenshire, and the miners and tin workers of the Swansea Valley. Furthermore, the style of these four master short-story writers is familiar to us all: it is the classic and traditional style of the short story in England, France, Russia, America, a style that has produced many masterpieces and will certainly be the medium for many more.

And now here you are, John Gwilym Jones, author of 'Y Goeden Eirin' and five other stories, come to break new ground in the Welsh language. Your characters are Welsh to the marrow of their bones, devout people and chapel-goers, who know their Bible as our forefathers did, but it is not possible to locate them in any specific district. There is no picture of any particular corner of Wales in your stories. It is not possible to show on any map where the Plum Tree grows. Is that correct, and if so, why?

In one sense the statement is true, though I must admit that realising it came as a bit of a shock to me. I think of almost all my characters either as farmers or quarrymen – the two occupations with which I'm most familiar – although I'm afraid I must acknowledge that it can't be claimed there is any essential connection between the characters in my stories and the work they do. They aren't what they are because they're farmers or quarrymen. Their social and economic status has hardly anything to do with the way they think. Having to realise that was a shock because, most definitely, every one of the stories has a particular part of Caernarfonshire – the parish of Llandwrog[2] – as its setting.

It's there I see everything happening. I've tried to describe the fields, streams, rivers, hills, houses and chapels of the district, and I've called them by their real names too. The Plum Tree was a very special plum tree. I don't know whether anyone ever fell out of its topmost branches, but I climbed it hundreds of times. It's no longer there, unfortunately, but I could show you the exact spot where it once stood. It grew precisely where it's said to grow in the story.

Of course, I'm aware that I have no right to expect anyone, apart from those who live there, to recognize the parish of Llandwrog from the references to it in the stories, nor can I hope to persuade anyone that Absalom and Glyn and John Llywelyn and Gwen Jones think as they do just because they were born and brought up there, went to particular chapels and heard particular preachers and men praying, attended particular schools and were taught by particular teachers. After all, I wasn't describing Llandwrog for its own sake, but making use of it. The district was to hand, as it were, and I was familiar with it. It was a convenient rather than a necessary setting. The Plum Tree, too, was a useful symbol for showing the small, superficially trivial things that drive one man in a certain direction and his neighbour in another.

May I move on to the second point, that the style and structure of your stories are unfamiliar. There has been some complaint on this score in the papers, to the effect that you were not writing for the common people. There are two parts to this complaint. Enid touches on one in the story 'The Stepping Stones' – I shall come back to that in a moment. Do you know what the second part is? One reason why your style is difficult is that it is too Welsh. Your characters have too much Welsh culture, too much Welsh literature in their memory and consciousness for Welsh readers to be able to understand them. If a character in one of your stories is fanciful, he refers to the horned ram and Morus the Wind and the figures in Welsh nursery rhymes.[3] If a girl feels romantic, she imagines herself to be like the Maid of Cefn

Ydfa marrying Maddocks.[4] *A romantic lad reads the Grail and the Mabinogion.*[5] *All your characters have read Daniel Owen and Dafydd ap Gwilym, Ann Griffiths and Williams Parry, the Llywarch Hen sequence and Pantycelyn, and they bring all these into their thoughts and speech.*[6] *You describe a child of unknown parentage thus: "He was, like the contemporary literature of Wales, pitifully ignorant of his lineage".*[7] *Now that's an odd and unexpected comparison!*

I'd much rather you hadn't asked that question, but it would be cowardly of me not to answer it. I know many teachers share my conviction on this point, so I venture to make a suggestion. There's a widespread belief nowadays that every child has a right to the same opportunity and amenities as every other child. No one in his right senses would disagree with that – all children should have an equal opportunity. But it's merely sentimental to believe that every child is able to make the same use of his opportunity. The truth is – an unpalatable truth, perhaps, but nevertheless the truth – that far more children than many people are willing to admit are wholly unable to make full use of the education that's available to them. No sensible teacher thinks less of his pupils just because they fail, but he would be deceiving himself if he refused to face the fact. Not even the most able teacher can hope to succeed in taking a substantial number of his pupils along the road that eventually turns them into men and women who are capable of enjoying the poems of Dafydd ap Gwilym and the prose of Morgan Llwyd, the sonnets of Williams Parry and the essays of Parry Williams,[8] the music of Bach and the paintings of Van Gogh. It's not fair to say they are worthless members of their communities on that account. They can be very useful, and they are. But nor is it fair to say that Bach should not have composed his music, nor Van Gogh painted his pictures, nor Williams Parry written his sonnets just because many people can never hope to understand and appreciate them.

There's a large number of people who are capable of enjoying literature and yet they complain that what is called a modern style is too consciously difficult for them to understand. I am very willing to acknowledge that some writers make a virtue of their obscurity, but at the same time it should be remembered that simplicity in itself is not a virtue. As readers many of us, I fear, are lazy, expecting to understand everything at the first reading. There are plenty of examples of great works that can be understood at the first reading, but that is certainly not the secret of their greatness. I wonder whether we in Wales today are content with a superficial knowledge of everything? It can be seen in the theatre and in what we read. We insist on walking before we're able to crawl and expect to derive pleasure without having prepared ourselves for it. We are too spineless to engage with anything. Laurence Olivier, for example, didn't come to an understanding of King Lear, and to give an interpretation of him that will never be forgotten by those who saw it, after one reading. No one who really loves poetry reads it as something to while away the time, but as something to take pains with, just as the author took pains in writing it. It's fair to expect those who claim to love poetry to have steeped themselves in the literature of Wales all their lives, and to be able to decide the worth of any new work in the light of that knowledge.

That raises another point. Can you say which Welsh writers have had an influence on your work? What is your connection with the contemporary literature of Wales?

Well, one of the things that gave me most enjoyment as a child was the Sunday preacher who used to come to my home for tea. It provided me with a splendid opportunity of comparing his real voice, his ordinary voice, with the one he used in the pulpit to preach and give out the hymns. I'm almost certain it was from this awareness of many a preacher's two voices – not that there was anything wrong in it – that I came to feel each one of us leads a very different life on his own from the life he shows to other people. This nurtured in me a desire to portray the personal life of characters when they had only a very weak censor to inhibit them from telling the truth about themselves, not to other people, but to themselves. I have to be honest and admit that I began to practise the Plum Tree style only after failing to write stories in what you call 'the classic and traditonal style of the short story'. I tried my best, but my stories were only lifeless, rough imitations of the work of Kate Roberts. It became quite clear to me that I had neither the skill nor the talent nor the necessary sympathy with the quarrymen of my home district to do justice to their courage and fortitude. There was nothing for it but to be content with the style that was easier for me and more in keeping with my own nature. You notice I say 'to be content', for I believe the ability to write a story about exterior, objective events is superior to analysis of the human mind, in the same way as tragedy is superior to comedy. The writers who helped me most were English and American and, in translation, French – Virginia Woolf, Hemingway, Saroyan, Sherwood Anderson, Proust. I read Joyce's *Dubliners* and his *Portrait of the Artist as a Young Man* years ago, but only recently, after writing *Y Goeden Eirin*, did I acquire a copy of *Ulysses*.[9]

Some of these writers, Sherwood Anderson, for instance, describe a state of mind and the actions of characters which in some way or other are abnormal. I tried to do the same in two of the stories, but my principal aim was to deal with thoughts that are to all intents and purposes completely normal, to deal with the difficulties and duality and conflicts that seem to me to be common to most of us. It wasn't at all difficult to make the setting Welsh because I'm a Welshman who is very conscious of his Welshness. I could do no other; it was inevitable.

But again, what about the influence of Welsh literature?

Although most of the stories in Welsh literature weren't much help, my debt to the Sleeping Bard, *Llythyr i'r Cymru Cariadus* and *Llyfr y Tri Aderyn* is immense.[10] I used to read parts of them and make lists of words and idioms with which I was unfamiliar, and then I'd make myself compose, on any subject under the sun, sentences that included a certain number of the new words and idioms. Then I'd take whole sentences and deconstruct them and make new sentences on exactly the same pattern. Then I'd choose a paragraph and imitate it, clause by clause, simile by simile, repeating it again and again, antithesis by antithesis – in short, doing what Robert Louis Stevenson[11] calls 'playing the sedulous ape' – hoping something like a personal style would develop out of the exercise.

I can't give any sort of date for when I began reading modern

English writers, but it was at some time after I'd left College. I've never gone in for systematic reading – I just read all sorts of things in Welsh and English, willy-nilly, whatever came to hand, sometimes having two or three books on the go at one and the same time. I don't have a good memory and what remains with me is a very general impression of the books I read – an impression of form and structure rather than of detail. I could never write a book that relies on facts, and that's another reason why I chose the easier path. Following the course of a character's mind lends itself to the imagination. Anything can come into a man's mind – I rely on neither place nor time – and no one can doubt the accuracy of it in the way the accuracy of description of external things can often be doubted.

As a result of this unsystematic reading I identified the style that gives me pleasure. I prefer a symbol to direct description – things like the poetry of Blake and the rhymes of Parry-Williams that are superficially simple, but which in fact are rich quarries, writing that insists on the reader's doing half the work, instead of being spoon-fed.

Literature is something that gives pleasure, no one denies that. But perhaps a false meaning is given to the word 'pleasure' when it's explained as some sort of sensual langour, instead of considering it as a stimulus to make a man think, to make him all ears and eyes. That's why I believe the study of contemporary poetry in Welsh and English does children good. Admittedly, it's often difficult to understand, but as children get to grips with it they realise literature is something that deserves their whole absorption and not just dreamy music with which they are coaxed to sleep.

You know, you are almost taking me away from the short story to talk about the teaching of literature in schools, and that's a subject I feel very strongly about. But I have to go back to the second difference between your stories and those of your predecessors. Enid complains to Absalom: "I'm fed up with these stories that have no structure to them, that presuppose an idea and Freudian analysis are sufficient to create literature", and yet she goes on to complain that your characters, in expressing their thoughts, mix their past and present and future into one incomprehensible mess.[12] Will you say something about

*the difficulty that many, apart from Enid, have found in your stories
and try to guide them through the labyrinth?*

The only answer I can give to that question lies in the question
itself. The beginning of the story from which you quote is, for
better or for worse, a kind of apology for the form it takes. It
seems to me that every reader, somehow or other, has to decide
what the author's aims are, and judge his work in the light of
those aims. For example, Jane Austen lived during the
Napoleonic wars, and yet in her novels she chose to ignore them
completely. It wasn't her aim to demonstrate her district's
response to those wars, but rather to draw a portrait of the snob-
bish, superficial life of the society in which she lived, and to find
husbands for her young women. That was her range and she was
canny enough to restrict herself to it, for every author fails when
he tries to step outside his own boundaries. No one has the right
to blame Jane Austen for doing to Napoleon what Nelson did to
him.[13] As I confessed earlier, writing a story in which incident
follows incident in chronological order – in other words, a story
with an acceptable plan to it – is completely beyond me. I had to
face up to that. I had skipped through the works of some recent
psychologists and read stories and novels that obviously made
use of new discoveries in the field. I found myself taking pleasure, and perhaps giving pleasure to others, in imagining
characters and gallivanting in their minds.

Everyone knows that neither place nor time puts any limit on
the mind. One minute we can be perspiring in the heat of the
tropics and, the next, freezing at the poles. One moment we're
remembering a piece of chocolate that someone gave us in
Caernarfon thirty years ago and, the next, wondering what
there'll be for supper tonight. Everyone, I'm sure, at some time
or another, has heard someone say on the way home from
chapel, after a boring sermon, perhaps, 'I've been everywhere
this morning'. I tried to follow the mind on its journey to those
various places, with ideas hard on the heels of other ideas
without much connection between them.

Do you mean the study of psychology has changed the development of the novel and the short story for ever, and if so, what kind of difference?

The contribution of recent psychology has probably been to help mankind to a better understanding of himself and his motives.

Ever since the Renaissance and the Protestant Reformation man's interest in himself has grown and deepened. That's what a writer is – a man who believes his own response and personal experience are sufficiently valuable and interesting to give pleasure to others. Writers have always been like that, except that writers of the last four hundred years have been less shy of talking about themselves. But although some of the shyness has disappeared, writers haven't been willing to tell the whole truth – there was still a part of their personality that was to be kept hidden. To talk of some things – sex in particular – was to offend against good taste and therefore unartistic. This belief is very much alive in Wales today.

What about Freud's influence?

Freud and his disciples have revealed that each one of us has a bottomless well in our subconscious and unconscious, and that we are often driven by tendencies and motives over which we have no control. Now I am very, very willing to acknowledge that a good deal of nonsense is talked about these hidden motives, but it's not all nonsense. It seems to me that any novelist who refuses to consider this new knowledge will fail to present a rounded, truly complete portrait of a person's character.

But while accepting that writers have a right to speak about anything without restriction, great care must be taken. The inclusion of coarse things just for the sake of including them breaks the basic rules of all literature worthy of the name. Unless their inclusion adds something wholly necessary to a portrait, they should be omitted. The other day I met a friend who referred to the Plum Tree. This friend isn't old-fashioned, but a man with a broad mind, his knowledge of Welsh, English and continental literature deep and wide-ranging. He gave me his opinion that some of the observations in the stories could have been left out without prejudice to their quality. Naturally I couldn't agree with him, or I wouldn't have written them in the way I did. But perhaps he's right and my instinct isn't yet fine enough to sense some things that are unartistic.

May I put another question to you and ask you to go into some detail to help readers to understand your kind of story: how does a short story grow in your mind – do you start with an idea?

Every story I've written grew out of an idea that was ambiguous and vague at first. Often a sentence in a book would suggest it, or sometimes what someone among my acquaintances had said or done. Although I mulled it over and over in my mind, it continued to be vague. I usually had some rough idea about the shape the story was to take – its beginning and its middle and its end — and sometimes I was able to form the first sentence without having to write it down on paper, but no further than that. The act of writing alone ensured that the story grew. The act of writing a word on paper, and seeing it in front of me, somehow suggested another word and that, in turn, suggested an idea. Often I had to change the form I'd decided on at the outset because a corgi of an idea had stuck its nose in and made a mess of everything.

Reading the story after finishing it was a very strange experience. I couldn't believe it was I who'd written it, it was so unfamiliar. I'm not suggesting the story had written itself – nothing of the sort. Writing is for me difficult and troublesome work and I have to be wide awake while making the effort. Reading the story, I was aware that everything that had been written had gone through my mind at one time or another. What surprised me was the whole caboodle had come together, into the one place, and had created a character who in one respect bore some resemblance to me and yet, in truth, was completely unlike me. This realisation makes me doubt whether writers like Virginia Woolf and Hemingway and Saroyan, who choose to write about the course of the human mind, have created wholly objective characters. Is not every one of their characters part of themselves? In writing these stories, my ambition and wish was to make them completely and thoroughly Welsh in spirit. The young people of every country analyse themselves, but I wanted my characters to analyse themselves as Welsh people nurtured on the literature and nonconformity of Wales. I envied English writers who could take advantage of those who had preceded them, quoting from their work in the knowledge that there were enough readers to recognize the quotations and respond to them. I tried my best to imitate them by quoting from our own literature. I hoped by means of that Welsh literary background to make a red-blooded Welsh person of all my characters. I also hoped to be able to write a book that would be the inevitable consequence of everything that had gone before it, and that depended on its predecessors as a child on its parents.

Yes, that is what I said earlier, that your characters have so much Welsh culture that they are odd and strange to Welsh readers, who find them difficult to understand. But you have written plays and a novel as well as stories. I wonder whether there is a large difference between a play and the kind of story found in Y Goeden Eirin? *How did you come to write so variously?*

I don't think there's as much difference between plays and stories like those in *Y Goeden Eirin* as your question implies. What, after all, are the soliloquies of Macbeth and Hamlet other than Shakespeare's way of showing characters analysing themselves and dealing with their motives? Everyone who's fond of the theatre is prepared to accept the conventions of the stage. An audience in Elizabethan times was willing to listen to Hamlet talking to himself and in verse – two completely unnatural things. They didn't ask for realism in the scenes any more than in the costumes and the language used. The tendency of drama in England and Wales since then has been to imitate life – a room on stage is made as like a room in a house as it is possible to be, and everyday language is used. One consequence of this copying is that audiences are no longer willing to accept things like the 'asides' of the 18th century. They are prepared to accept a man talking to himself in verse but consider anyone talking to himself in ordinary language as ridiculously unnatural.

T.S. Eliot has realised that. In order to get people to accept the convention once again, and be content to listen to characters analysing themselves, he wrote *Murder in the Cathedral* and *A*

Family Reunion in verse. In order not to tax the audience too much, however, instead of having Thomas, the Archbishop, talking to himself, the author has devised four tempters to argue with him about his motives and intentions.

I believe it is possible, if only enough trouble is taken to write dialogue that is well-wrought verse or prose, to achieve on stage an analysis in the narrow sense given to that word by psychologists.

But short-story writers or novelists cannot do that exactly. They can convey mental confusion and one idea following on from another with no obvious connection between them for the simple reason that their readers, if they so choose, can read them for a second and a third time. A dramatist, on the other hand, has to drive the nail home with a single blow. He has to be more formal, simpler, less circumlocutory. He does not have the same chance to draw an accurate picture of the twisting, wholly fantastic paths that our thoughts take.

You are again raising interesting matters, but before we end – would you say the company and conversation of writers and artists has spurred you into writing? Have they had any part in your work?

Unfortunately, I was never lucky enough to meet and have long conversations with writers and artists of any standing.

During my time at College I happened to belong, at a distance, as it were, to a quite interesting circle who went in for talk about literature, but I didn't at that time have either the background or the knowledge to make proper use of it. Since then, very occasionally, I have had an opportunity of talking to writers, but far too infrequently for it to be of any worth; and I must be honest and confess that I find it very difficult to talk profoundly, or to take myself seriously. But I have a few very close friends, some of whom are writers, who have always been kind and patient enough to read or listen to my work, and sincere enough to express an opinion of it. I can't say how much I owe them for their criticism and encouragement. Going to the theatre and reading literary criticism and novels and a little psychology have done more to awaken my interest in literature than talking to others.

I must thank you for our talk which, I hope, will show our listeners how a book like Y Goeden Eirin *came to be written. I don't think anyone who has heard you will any longer believe that it was some attempt to be strange or clever which accounts for the style of your stories. They grow in the only way and in the only form that is possible for them, and their style and form give new life to the short story in Welsh and demonstrate how much is still possible in the language. I first came across your work at the Eisteddfod held in Denbigh in 1939.[14] I knew then that an accomplished writer had emerged. I must thank you for your talent. Welsh literature's need today is to have men and women prepared and able seriously to devote their minds and creative energy and determination to enriching and renewing her youth. Literature is a discipline, the discipline of a lifetime. There is too little of that in Wales these days.*

Decline

First light one morning on a day in Spring, which had come early. The sun shone feebly like a tallow candle in a large room. The sheep stood about as if half asleep, their lambs sucking vigorously, the milk coursing down their throats and their breath like that of long-distance runners.

The sun was now high enough in the sky to shine in through the bedroom windows of Garreg Wen.

Its rays illuminated the patchwork quilt on the bed, the colours lighting up one after another – red and yellow, blue and mauve and white – the wedding dress of Elin Gruffydd, and her mother's Paisley shawl in which Meredydd had been swaddled as a baby.

Meredydd gave a racking cough, cold and dry, which shook his whole body. Turning on his right side, he coughed again. He sat up in bed, his mop of black hair making his pale face seem even paler.

His arms were so thin that his hands and long nails seemed too heavy for them. The bones of his wrists stood out and his skin was creased like the dried pelt of an animal.

There was warm sweat on his face and hands; not wholesome sweat, but like the steam from a kettle when it turns into water on a glass held before it. His eyes, black as damsons, restless as wild birds in a cage, were filled with despair and thwarted ambition.

Presently, life came into them. They sparkled. The pale cheeks turned an unnatural red, and he began to run his long, thin, sensitive fingers over the quilt. They moved from one colour to another, from red to white, from blue to mauve, and back to red. He raised his arms and then brought them down as if striking a chord. Then he ran the fingers of his right hand to the edge of the bed as if playing a long sequence, now with his left hand, then with both. He smiled, revealing a row of white teeth, his whole body moving in time with the song in his head.

Suddenly he stopped, drained of all vivacity. The smile vanished, and in its place his jaw was clenched, his lips bloodless. His eyes were eloquent with the sadness of unfulfilled hopes, with the disappointment of a life which had not achieved its goal, a broken heart, despair.

The hands were once more lowered and the fingers played again across the coverlet, slowly and lightly now as if drawing music from the colours, one that spoke of pain and anguish and loss. He looked out of the window and saw, in the field, a lamb gambolling at the side of its mother, which stopped grazing to allow it to suck her milk. He fell back onto his pillow.

'Mam!'

'Yes, my boy?'

Hardly had he shouted than he heard a sound on the stone flags of the kitchen. Elin took off her clogs at the bottom of the stairs and came up in her stockinged feet for the umpteenth time that morning.

'Yes, my boy, what do you want?'

'Nothing, Mam.'

It was always the same. She was at his beck and call and yet he never wanted anything. For a moment a wave of weariness came over her face. She closed her eyes, her eyelids heavy from lack of sleep. She ran a hand across her brow, sat down on the bedside chair, and thought, and thought, and thought.

The disease that was rapidly killing Meredydd was no less effectively making her grow old. The last few months had taken their toll, for she had insisted on tending him herself, and in her foolish pride refusing all help from neighbours.

She had been thirty-five at the time of her marriage to William Gruffydd of Garreg Wen, and they had married against the wishes of her parents.

'The man's in decline, and so was his family before him.'

'You'll have children to think about, my girl.'

But her father's efforts had been in vain, as had her mother's pleading; for wasn't William Gruffydd the owner of Garreg Wen, and hadn't his father, and his bachelor uncle, left him a lot of money? Her clothes and linen would be as good as those of Mary Ellis and her house and furniture as neat as those of Alis Williams of Ty Mawr. In the early years of their marriage she found no cause for regret.

After three years they had a child and called him Meredydd, but within a few months William Gruffydd's back was bent and he expired, in the end, like a snuffed candle. There, hanging above Meredydd's bed, was his epitaph: *In memory of William*

Gruffydd, the husband of Elin Gruffydd, who died on March 28, 1898, at the age of 41.

But now she had Garreg Wen, money in the bank, and Meredydd, her child – and his father's too.

She recalled her father's words and decided that, come what may, she would prove him wrong. She spared neither cost nor effort, but gave the boy everything that was in her power to give. One day, some day, Meredydd Gruffydd would be as strong, as robust, as physically fit as any man in the district, a support for his mother, incontrovertible proof that her marriage had not been a mistake. She had given him an education, and one day he would pay her back. Many a time she imagined herself in Caernarfon of a Saturday morning and meeting Mary Ellis, perhaps, or Alis Williams.

'Hello, Elin, how are you today?'

'Quite well, thank you.'

'You're out early.'

'Yes, I'm on my way to the bank.'

'The bank?'

'Yes, my Meredydd's so good to me, you know. No lad was ever better to his mother.'

She kept her resolve. Meredydd left elementary school for the county school, and great was his teachers' praise of him.

She sent him for music lessons, and he grew fond of the subject. He was very clever at examinations and so successful that she decided to send him to the Royal Academy of Music in London.

They were three anxious and expensive years for her, but not a week passed without her managing to send him money and a parcel with two pounds of home-made butter and clean, warm clothes in it. The London air was not as keen and healthy as that of Llan y Groes, and he needed butter to put marrow in his bones. He wrote to her, and her heart leapt as she read some of his letters, so clear and bright did his future seem.

> Dear Mother,
> Thank you for the letter and money and parcel... and he told me I was sure to win the prize... This evening I shall be playing at the College concert... I was top of the class, with 98 marks out of 100.

She expected that after Meredydd had finished his course in the capital he would return home to give music lessons to the village children, play the piano in this concert and that eisteddfod, and then become an adjudicator. It was only a momentary disappointment when she realized how far superior Meredydd's excellence was to her own unsophisticated expectations.

He stayed on in London. He gave concerts at the Queen's Hall, where his mother was able to come and hear him, sitting in the front stalls, enjoying the thunderous applause for her son, who was no longer his father's, for had not all the poison he had inherited from William Gruffydd been washed out of his system by her solicitude?

She recalled the morning when a picture of Meredydd had appeared in *The Daily Sketch* with a caption to the effect that he had been invited to play the piano in the presence of the king. There was nothing else she needed from the shop but that was where she went.

'Did you see this, Williams?'

'Well, 'pon my word, it's Meredydd! You must be very proud of him.'

Proud!

After that, it was not such a happy time. The letters did not arrive with the same regularity, though they continued to bring news of Meredydd's success. Then, one morning Elin realized with horror that her son would not be spending his summer holidays at Garreg Wen. He was to visit the continent in the company of friends.

'Perhaps,' he wrote, 'this will do me more good. I had a cold recently and I just can't get rid of it. Working too hard, maybe.'

A cold! Unable to get rid of it! But no, that was quite natural with him working so hard. The following Christmas he came home, thinner, perhaps, though not enough to cause her too much anxiety, but for the next two years she did not see him at all. She received a letter from time to time, sometimes posted from London, sometimes Paris or some other city on the continent. The villagers gossiped but Elin went on holding her head high. She was not done yet.

Six months ago Meredydd arrived home one evening and when his mother set eyes on him her heart sank. His breath came in gasps and the colour had drained from his cheeks; whenever someone spoke to him he trembled, and with every day that passed his eyes sank deeper into his head.

Elin did not blame him. Rather, she blamed herself. She had failed; his father had triumphed; all that was left for her now was to try and do her best for the boy who ought never to have been born. She fetched and carried for him, obeyed his every whim... Perhaps... who knows? While's there's life there's hope.

Meredydd had some good days. He would enjoy his food, slept soundly, and on those occasions Elin would pray in her heart: 'O Lord, restore Meredydd's strength. Let him be healthy and go to London again and send his mother letters. Let not my efforts be in vain.'

But more often she would be downhearted. He coughed, was unable to get his breath, tossed and turned in his sleep, muttered to himself, and many was the time she tried to understand what he was saying with her ear at his lips and his warm breath on her face. Then she would pray: 'O Lord, release him, and grant me forgiveness.'

Today was one of those days, and as she sat at his bedside Meredydd slipped into a fitful sleep: he threw the bedclothes off him, waved his hands, and coughed. He also talked, not incomprehensibly now but in a hoarse voice, like a man intoxicated: 'Red wine... red wine... a lovely body... wine... Waiter, waiter, two benedictines... one for you and one for me... Maria... wine... Stop drinking, did you say, doctor?...'; he laughed uncontrollably.

Elin got to her feet and clenched her fist so tightly that she drew blood, but without feeling the pain. She managed not to scream, and quickly wiped away the tears that welled in her eyes. She straightened up with hatred on her face. After all the hoping, all the dreaming, all the sacrifice, this. After the taste of success and fame, this. Agitated by what she was feeling, she almost ran downstairs, collapsed into an armchair and wept, like a lonely bird that has lost its mate, her heart broken.

'Mam!'

She stopped crying at once. How dare he, having misled her so, having shattered her dreams, and let her scurry about, day and night, carrying out his every whim?

'Mam! Mam!'

No, she could not. Let him call. A mother's love cannot be expected to forgive such deceit and treachery. How could she look at him without showing her hatred?

'Mam!'

There was silence for a moment; then Elin looked up. Her eyes filled again with hot tears, and as if struggling with something stronger than herself, and slowly overcoming it and bringing it under control, she got up and made her way slowly to the foot of the stairs. Her breath came in deep gasps and her tears nearly blinded her.

'Yes, my boy, what do you want?'

'Nothing, Mam.'

Y Ford Gron (cyf.1, rhif 8, Mehefin 1931)

The Wedding

'We are gathered here together in the sight of God to join together this man and this woman in holy matrimony...' Like the marriage service, I am dignified enough, simple and unassuming, but painfully formal. Having recited it so many times has made it, for me, as mechanical as my prayers and the burial service. I can easily say one thing while thinking about something completely different. In an unguarded moment I might speak about the persons here present putting on immortality. I have often wondered what would happen if, instead of asking, 'So-and-so, wilt thou have this man to thy wedded husband?', I said, 'So-and-so, wilt thou have this man's heart?', and she sang out, 'I will, straightawa-a-y, my hea-eart's always belonged to Hy-y-wel.'[1] And at those rash moments, I feel like a flibbertigibbet. But this is how things are and thus they will remain.

I am as I am, too, and this is how I shall be from now on. I am deep in the rut and think of everything as a preamble and three heads. Presently I shall be giving these two persons advice. I shall start by speaking about the wedding in Cana of Galilee[2] and the Lord Jesus's interest in the small pleasures of the children of men. I shall mention first the need to pull together in the wedded state; secondly, about the opportunities for the enrichment of both partners in the wedded state; thirdly and lastly, about how it is proper to give pride of place in the wedded state to God, the Great Reality. From now on I shall have to be content, like the ploughshare, with the furrow. Only the crude, superficial experiences common to thousands of people will come my way. I hear the high wind and heavy rain. I see the highest peaks and the wide rivers. I have left behind the morning of my life with its zephyrs and daisies. I am now in the sullen afternoon with its moon-daisies. I have grown a thick skin against insult here and censure there. I have learned to bite my tongue before answering back. I move between the bickering deacons and the death-rattle of my flock. In trying to keep things on an even keel I have lost my own balance. I am like Pavlov's dogs, responding by conditioned reflex to a certain sound at specific times.[3] 'Earth to earth, ashes to ashes,' goes my voice automatically and my face composes itself in the lachrymose expression expected of it. 'I baptize thee, Peris Wyn,' goes my voice, and my face forms a smile of its own accord... 'This is my body, This is my blood,' goes my voice, and I am clad from head to foot in the necessary, conventional gravity...

And yet, when John Llywelyn's letter arrived... 'It was you who christened us both and received us as members of the church, and we should like you to marry us...', I could not but be proud. I felt as if my life had not been wholly in vain. Weaned of the ambition of youth, its visions and hopes and joys, I grew into the lukewarm, quotidian ordinariness of a good minister of Jesus Christ, and became content with my lot. This is my cross; but under its weight I have felt as much earthly happiness as is possible and just for the likes of me. I have been faithful in a few things, and I know that some day I shall enter into the joy of my Lord.

'Who giveth this woman to be married to this man?'

'I do.' And good riddance to her. I take a step forward, squaring my shoulders lest that wife of mine or Wil, my brother, or any of the relatives the pleasure of whose company we requested should think I care two hoots for any of them. Tonight I shall go to Davy John's shop and say, 'Two ounces of shag, Davy John.' 'Two ounces?' he will ask, stressing the word 'two' as if he were reciting. 'Yes, two,' I shall reply, my emphasis fully the equal of his, throwing down my money like a lord at a racetrack. And next week I shall buy three ounces. The butter, tea and sugar will last longer with only three mouths to feed instead of four. The week after that I shall buy a new pair of shoes. Before the month's out, I shall go to GG.'s shop in town to be measured for a pin-striped suit. 'How about this one?' I shall ask my brother, Wil, in a casual way. In less than a year I shall be offering my baccy to Jones, the quarry steward. 'Take a pipeful, Mr Jones?' 'I don't smoke shag.' 'Neither do I...'

'Catrin, where's my stud?' 'How should I know? Where did you put it?' 'If Lizzie Mary were here she'd soon find her father's stud'... 'This rice pudding isn't as good as usual.' 'Isn't it?' 'Far too watery.' 'I haven't made any for years. Lizzie Mary usually saw to that.'... 'Catrin, did you bring the *Faner*?'⁴ 'Drat it all, I forgot.' 'Lizzie Mary never forgot her father's newspaper of a

Wednesday evening.'... Well, as Twm Yes-and-No always main-
tains at the Literary Society, there's so much to be said on both
sides that I can't make up my mind. I think I'll abstain.

'John Llywelyn Evans. Wilt thou have this woman to thy
wedded wife?'

'I will.' The organ pipes are arranged neatly according to their
size, those at both ends looking so tall and stout because the ones
in the middle are so short. It's a comparative matter. And somewhere in the middle there are another two, though I can't say for
sure whether either is the taller. If Mr Lewis made sounds come
out of them there would be at least half a tone between them, and
my ear would notice the difference.

I should like to be a critic and able to list the books of the ages
in order of merit. That's not possible, of course. It would not be
difficult to choose the books at either end. My large pipes would
be the Bible and the Mabinogi.[5] 'Yes,' my critics would say, 'we
are quite happy to have the Bible at one end, but why the
Mabinogi? Have you not heard of Euripides and Tacitus and
Shakespeare and Cervantes and Dante and Balzac and Tolstoy
and Goethe and... ?' 'Of course I have, I've heard of them all, but
I'm a Welshman.' 'Ah,' they would say pedantically, 'literature is
above nationality. You mustn't think within the limits of your own
country; you have to reach out, widen your horizons and see
author and book in their proper place as part of the development
of world literature; you must acquire a classical mind and learn
how to compare and contrast and discover how much an author
learned from those who went before him. Then decide whether
he added anything or merely lived off the riches of his forebears.
A good critic has to know where lyric and novel come from.
They're not made of nothing, hovering in the air and unconnected as gossamer. It's mere romanticism to think like that,
criticism that is nothing but personal taste or whim.'

And I know deep down that all their arguments have a cruel
logic. Even so, there's no argument in the whole wide world that
would topple the Mabinogi from its pedestal. Myfanwy and
Ceridwen and Eluned have prettier names than Lizzie Mary.
Perhaps Miss Davies County School knows more about cooking
than Lizzie Mary. Jane Ty Gwyn is of sweeter temper and Megan
Ty Capel has better manners. Lizzie Mary, I readily concede, has

a mind formed by reading English penny dreadfuls and tabloid newspapers and watching Hollywood films. She hasn't a clue about politics or literature, and in neither do Reaction and Revolt mean anything to her. But she is my darling, and that's all that matters. Will I take this woman to my wedded wife? I will, straightawa-a-y, my heart has always belonged to Li-i-zzie. You'd be scared out of your wits if she sang out like that, wouldn't you, Edward Jones? You'd be surprised how near I am to doing so. Now Lizzie Mary hands her bouquet to her sister, Gwen, and Robin has his finger and thumb in his waistcoat pocket, fumbling for the ring. He's very fond of the Mabinogi, too. Poor Robin!

'Lizzie Mary Jones, wilt thou have this man to thy wedded husband...?'

'I will.' There, I've said the words simply, flatly, with no more than the reasonable excitement of any bride. I never imagined my wedding would be like this. There was a time when I imagined myself a foolish young man's fancy. I'd wander with him through the white wheat and stroll along the sheep-walks until we reached the green grass. But in the end, after many tribulations, after suffering the brutishness of my parents, having written in blood from my own arm, I was forced to stand beside Maddocks in the church, wretched as a wilting lily. Behind me sat my proud family; at my side the haughty Maddocks wed my body, and somewhere out there was Wil, breaking his heart. Don't break your heart, Wil. Before long the Maid of Cefn Ydfa[6] will be lying quietly in the churchyard, and all Wales will be singing your pastoral song... .

Once I imagined myself saying, 'I will,' and trembling with burning passion. At my side stood a fine figure of a man, a man amongst men, like Clark Gable in *He Adored Her*.[7] He had one of those rugged, attractive faces, sleek hair and a devil-may-care little twist to the corner of his mouth. I enjoyed humiliating him and bewitching him into saying 'I will' so gratefully, so humbly; yet the touch of his hand on mine as he put the ring on my finger made me flesh, every inch of me. I stood there with brazen face and abstractions like morality and chastity and moderation had ceased to be, and even quite tangible things like my father's scowl and the back of mother's hand and the tongue of Betsan

Jones Next Door counted for nothing...

Another time I'd marry above my station. Behind sat my mother. 'A Triplex grate, wooden bedsteads, a three-piece suite and a carpet,' she would tell herself. 'I'm taking a fortnight's holiday this year,' my father would say to the quarry steward, 'to stay with my daughter at Bumford Hall.' 'I'm going to Paris,' my sister Gwen would say. 'To Paris?' 'Yes, with Lady Elizabeth.' 'Lady Elizabeth?' 'My sister, Lady Elizabeth Bumford, you know...' But this is what's happening. I'm marrying one of my own kind, without either having to or feeling any more than the usual thrill any woman feels on her wedding day. I say 'I will' quite simply, straightforwardly, and I'm perfectly content and perfectly happy it's the right and sensible thing to do.

'Then let the man put the ring on the fourth finger of the woman's left hand.'

There's the ring on her finger. Now I'm a man who covets his neighbour's wife, an adulterer in my mind, a prey to the unease and affliction of things half done, a soul without a body. I shall have bouts of lust without the forgiveness of lusting together, followed by drowsy, lonely torpor. And pain and guilt next morning; for I can never free myself from the chains of the Ten Commandments or the shackles of the thousand and one commandments of my own home. Thou shalt not commit adultery, nor bear false witness, nor play cards on a Sunday, nor put a shilling on a horse, nor touch strong drink. I do all these things gnawed by the traditional guilt of a child brought up in the Fellowship.[8] I was denied the enjoyment of sin and the short-sightedness that sees only the single act in isolation.

Last night I was tossing and turning for hours on end. Tonight will be worse. Trying to curb myself, I'll stretch and tauten all my muscles. I'll wrap myself into a ball with my arms tight around my legs and my chin on my knees. I'll pummel the pillows with the monotonous rhythm of a piston. I'll tire and, suddenly furious, turn again. Again and again I turn. And all the while the same thing will be going through my mind, dragging itself along and wallowing there like a toad in mire... But at this moment I am perfectly happy; indeed, more than happy. I can observe myself last night and tonight, and every night, entirely without emotion or prejudice, and see the loathing, not because the Old Testament and my mother taught me, but because a kind of mystical uplift, some kind of purification, has visited me. My mind has been scoured, and in this brief cleanliness I can observe myself last night and tonight as a stranger. I am more critical, see more clearly the futility and waste of energy. But they are the futility and waste of another man – not mine. Nurtured within me is the integrity of the good critic who sees faults impartially and notes them without malice. They are not my faults, so there is no call to make any resolutions. It does not fall to me to stifle the lust of another man who happened to be alive last night and will be again this evening.

I wonder whether it is in giving us this glimpse of the old man and allowing us to sense his strangeness that Jesus Christ forgives our sins? Such joy is very familiar to me. Something from without which forced itself in upon me... poetry, a good sermon, a Bach fugue, a logical argument, pictures, acting, a high mass that I once heard.

Today, the marriage covenant in accordance with God's holy ordinance. At my side, John Llywelyn shivering as he did long ago after we'd had an icy dip in Llyn Hafod Ifan, all pain without but warm with happiness and life within; Gwen, the sound of the service giving her drowsy eyes the happy look of the young when contemplating their end. I imagine her composing a sonnet – 'When my frail flesh is laid into the grave...'; old Edward Jones with his honest intonation turning this ring, and I do solemnly declare, and as ye shall answer at the dreadful day of judgement when the secrets of all hearts shall be disclosed, into a true act of worship. And in the fine breeze of this sanctification, I can gaze upon Lizzie Mary without coveting her, and can feel her closeness without wanton thoughts. This is the purification, the beauty absolute. It brings me forgiveness (don't mention that ten pounds ever again, Evan Hughes), and jocularity (you fell down, Huw *bach*, come here and let me pick you up), and humility (I am not worthy), and a bit of boasting too (I can do all things).

'Forasmuch as John Llywelyn Evans and Lizzie Mary Jones have consented together in holy wedlock...'

Today I'm seventeen years old. Dressed in blue silk, I stand in the deacons' seat at Penuel at the side of Lizzie Mary, my sister, who is surprisingly self-possessed in her white. I'm very,

very happy. Yesterday I was in school listening to Miss Rees grind out the old rigmarole. Her questions were as predictable as the cold sore on her lip. She keeps it as a souvenir of the Great War, in which she lost her sweetheart. Which mutation follows '*yn*'? Why is '*eu gilydd*' incorrect? What is 'anchoress'? Where is Sarras? Who was Moradrins?[9] Spinsterish things, barren as herself. But I don't want to think about her or the likes of her. I want to think about the adventurous and lovely things in my life... learning for the first time the difference between the male and female of the red campion; feeling the breeze that cools the scent of gorse; getting my feet wet in the Cae Doctor river and going all day with wet feet and not catching a cold; finding the nest of a hen that was laying out; being taken ill and people bringing me calf's foot jelly; shutting my eyes and wondering who will weep for me when I'm dead. Lizzie Mary's wedding-day will be among them. One day little Gwenhwyfar will be on my lap asking, 'Mam, what were the best things that ever happened to you?' and I'll reply, 'Well... finding a double-yoked egg... and your Aunt Lizzie Mary's wedding-day... and...'

What did I say? Little Gwenhwyfar? Mam? Today Lizzie Mary's taking a vow to become a mother. In our family tree her name will be coupled with John Llywelyn's. I hope one day I shall stand here in white silk. I shouldn't want to be like Queen Anne alone in her family tree. Though she had, to be sure, her cold sore... I am the Holy Grail.[10] I am the sacred vessel preserved by Joseph of Arimathea. Here I am, in the court of Pelles, the grandfather of Galahad, in all the splendour of my holiness, pure, intact, like the Virgin Mary, undefiled, immaculate. Who comes now on a pilgrimage from Arthur's court at Camelot? Who is this with a golden spur on his right foot? Burt? Lionel? Percival? Galahad? Come, my Galahad! Come, O predestined seeker of the Holy Grail. Loiter with hermits along the untrodden paths of dark forests, but come! Linger a while in the company of beautiful maidens in wooded valleys, but come! Deliver monks from their execrable bodies in their sacred burial-grounds, but come! Slay thy ten knights and slay thy forty, but come! Mourn at the funeral of Percival's sister, but come! Come, and I shall succour thee with my spiritual food, I shall show thee my secrets, I shall anoint thee king of my realm. Come! Come!

'And now the Reverend Arthur Davies will read a passage of Holy Scripture.'

'The Lord is my shepherd, I shall not want...' This is my first church and the first wedding since my induction, but I wasn't asked to officiate. I realize, of course, that memories and sentiment bind John Llywelyn and Lizzie Mary to their old minister, but for the life of me I can't help feeling offended. This is what happens to me. I've always taken second place. I come second with my mother because Robin, my brother, has a readier smile and is quicker to do a good turn. I was always second in my class at the County School for the simple reason that Bobi Tan-y-Wern was abler than me. At College, I got a second-class degree and was placed in the second division, and it was only after Rolant turned it down that I was offered this church. No one ever treats me unfairly. That's the trouble. If I were treated unfairly, it would be so much easier to be tolerant and content. Each time there are sufficient, understandable reasons why I should be set aside, and I see them myself and recognize how fair they are. Something always comes between me and fulfilment. I start everything in the knowledge that my success will be only moderate and for that reason I'm unable to throw myself body and soul into anything. One part of me does what it ought and the other just goes gadding about.

I should like to devote myself completely to my work... . to break through into mystical awareness like St. John of the Cross and Saint Theresa and Ann Griffiths.[11] Gwen Jones is an attractive little dish. To know the love that casteth out fear. How old is she, I wonder? That my soul might die unto itself to live in God. She's not too young. To walk in the light that makes things like the miraculous birth and the resurrection as natural as breathing and eating. There's passion in those sultry eyes. To swoon in heavenly bliss. And those full lips and firm breasts. Green pastures. Under a hedge... O Lord, why must I be tormented by this everlasting duality? Why must I be a beastly ram of sanctity and wantonness? Why can't I be either all body or all soul? Why can't my passions be given rein without the restraining power of Thy breath? Why can't my soul leap and dance free from the shackles of my desires? Why can't I be body-soul and soul-body, inseparable as a compound word? Why can't they appease and enliven each other? So that in following Thee I possess Gwen and in my lust for Gwen be in love with Thee? Such a thing is possible. I am determined to make it so... but who am I to insist on anything? I shall set out, like Percival, on an adventure. I shall walk through woods where birds sing. I shall fight with the serpent and see the ship with sails of white samite. I shall discourse with the man who bears the name Jesus Christ on his crown, and lose blood from the wound in my thigh. I shall reach the court of Pelles and my eyes shall behold the glory of the Holy Cup. But it is Galahad who shall see his adventure completed, Galahad, the predestined seeker, who will find his Holy Grail.

'And now may the grace of our Lord Jesus Christ and the love of God and the fellowship of the Holy Ghost be with you and remain with you this day and for ever more. Amen.'

Y Goedin Eirin (Gwasg Gee, 1946)

The Plum Tree

My brother Wil and I are twins. We were conceived at exactly the same moment, in the same place, and by the same love and the same desire. Mam ate the same food to give us both strength and felt the same pain while carrying us in her womb; we moved inside her at the same time and were born at the same time. The same hands brought us into the world and we were washed in the same water. We gave our mother the same fright and our father the same pride. We were put in the same cradle and suckled at the same breasts. The same hand rocked us and when we were weaned we ate from the same bowl. We followed each other around the floor like shadows one of the other, and exactly the same person taught us to say Mam and Dad and Sionyn and Wil and Taid and Nain[1] and bread-and-milk and pull-your-trousers-down and now-run-like-hell, and A for apple and B for baby, and who was the man beloved of God, and twice-one-is-two, and rest O wave, flow softly, don't clash against the rocks,[2] and drink of this cup for this is my blood, from the New Testament.

But today Wil, my brother, is in Egypt and I am working on the land at Maes Mawr.

For years I didn't realize there was any difference between us. Wil was Sionyn, Sionyn Wil. 'Sionyn, come here,' Mam would say, and Wil would run to her as fast as his little legs could carry him. 'Don't, Wil, you little rascal,' Dad would say, and I would obey instantly. When I was spanked and sent to bed without supper, Wil would undress as well and say his prayers and bawl his eyes out, his belly rumbling as we lay under the bedclothes; and when Wil sliced off the top of his thumb with a pair of scissors, there was blood on my thumb too, and I had it bandaged, just like Wil.

It was the plum tree in the garden that separated us. God planted it there.[3] And God said, Let there be a plum tree at the top of the garden at Llys Ynyr, between the privy and the wall; and so it came to pass. I'm not blaming God; I don't hold it against him. I'm quite willing to enjoy the good things he sends and we have to put up with the rest. God is responsible for the sun and moon and the stars and the sea and all that is within it, and the earth with its beasts, each after its own kind; cattle to give us calves and milk, and sheep to give us lambs and wool and warm clothes, and dogs to be our friends. It is to Him we must offer up our thanks for trees that bear fruit, each after its own kind; the oak to show us how to be strong and how to live to a ripe old age and to provide acorns for pigs; and apple trees that bear apples, some for eating and some for storing; and plum trees... small dark, shiny plums with the white stuff inside as sweet as honey, melting to leave between your tongue and palate a clean stone that can be spat out like a cork from a pop-gun. Yes, it was God planted the plum tree between the privy and the wall in our garden. I plant this, he said, to make Wil Wil and Sionyn Sionyn.

God is responsible for Man, too, having breathed life into his nostrils and created him in his own image. 'There you are, then,' He said, 'do as you like now. If you prefer someone to me, that's up to you. You can be Nebuchadnezzar[4] if you want, daft enough to eat grass, or you can be Daniel,[5] praying with your face towards Jerusalem. You can believe that I speak only to the Pope, or you can believe that Robin Puw, Ty Draw, knows me better than the Pope does. Bernard Shaw[6] thinks it's Robin Puw's and the Pope's imagination that makes them think I speak to them. You are welcome to believe that as well. Or, if you so wish, you can believe, like Stalin,[7] I'm a pretty little decoration, like a red flower on a tree, but that it's the tree which is important – that's what counts.'

But, God, that's not quite fair. Nebuchadnezzar, I admit, was a warmonger and a brute, but he made Babylon the world's most beautiful city of its day. True, Daniel was the epitome of a good boy, but he didn't lose a wink of sleep trying to alleviate the suffering of his fellow-slaves on the banks of the Euphrates. I don't know about the Pope, but I do know that Robin Puw is the father of little Neli Tai Cefn, though he won't admit it. Stalin's materialism did for five million peasants in the Ukraine, that's true, but he can't be wholly bad; just think of the fight the Russians are putting up at the moment. Don't think I've forgotten the plum tree in the garden; I haven't. God gave Wil the right to be Wil and me to be what I am, and although Wil has a sword and I a plough, Wil is a finer chap than me, and I think the world of Wil, and Wil thinks the world of me.

The plum tree was older than Nain. Although Nain is still alive, she was old even then, with deep lines on her face, yet healthy as a nut apart from her paralysed arm. She could deliver a good clout with her left hand, but her right was as useless as the weights of a long-case clock that has stopped. I used to think of Nain and the plum tree together. Both were alive before Gladstone[8] died and when Evan Roberts[9] was roaming the land and giving people strange experiences, some of which are still with us, may his blessed name be preserved, as John Huws Pant is fond of saying... We don't really know what Saviour and Mediator and Forgiveness and Repentance are, but we believe in them, and that's what matters...

I tend to take every opportunity of starting hares, so that I don't have to talk about the plum tree, I know that only too well, and with good reason. I hate having to think about it. I sometimes think of the plum tree as my worst enemy. It was the tree taught me that lifeless things like Nain's right arm are much more dangerous than live, healthy things like her left arm. The tree taught me that the Devil is in the world, and although it also taught me that nothing dies and everlasting life is an actual fact, I don't find that wholly comforting.

You have noticed that I mentioned lifeless things, and in the same breath I said that nothing dies. Inconsistent, you say. Perhaps so, indeed. A woolly mind. Equally true. Or perhaps words sometimes change their meaning according to their context. That's how Members of Parliament justify themselves, anyway. You're not being fair, they tell their critics, you're quoting out of context.

Once Wil and I went to see little Vaughan, the Bronallt boy, laid out in his coffin. By this time I knew Wil was Wil. We were no longer the one-in-two and the two-in-one; although we went there together, we were separate. Vaughan looked as if he were still alive: he had ruddy cheeks and his teeth looked as if he was smiling, and someone had given him a bunch of flowers to hold. His mother asked us did we know what was the last thing he had said:

> My little hen is a white little hen,
> Pink and yellow and red and black.

And I said to myself, Today he is a member of the United Choir of Paradise which astonishes the angels of glory with its blessed singing. I don't believe that today, mind you; that is, I don't believe precisely that. Perhaps Vaughan isn't singing, but he's doing something. I used to believe he was still alive because his mother and his sister Enid and I could remember him well. But his mother and Enid and I will die some time, and who will remember him then? And last week I read an article on Karl Barth[10], and I'm about to change my mind again.

That night, in bed, I heard Wil crying his eyes out. I put my arm around him. 'What's the matter, Wil?' I asked. 'Afraid of dying,' he said. 'Go to sleep in there,' said Mam. We were still one as far as she was concerned.

Today Wil is in Egypt because he's afraid of dying, and I am ploughing the fields of Maes Mawr because I know Wil is going to live for ever.

'Things are not too bad,' said Wil. 'Our standard of living is quite high. We have good food and plenty of it. And freedom.'

'Yes indeed,' I replied, 'at the expense of those who live in Africa and Malaya and India, whose standard of living is lower than that of any pig in this country. Just think of Krupp[11] in Germany and people like him over here.'

'It's easy for you to find fault with the rich,' said Wil. 'I know they cheat and starve the poor, but remember – our interests are the same as theirs. And what proof have you got that we'd be better off if coal, the railways and heavy industries were to be nationalized? What good would it do you, wearing yourself out trying to show society its own corruption? Good and bad, my boy, are so intermingled that you just can't draw a line between them, and our job is not to think of other people all the time, but to think more about our responsibility to ourselves, and to justify ourselves in our own eyes. And if someone prevents us from doing so, well, there's only one thing for it. You know, Sionyn, I haven't got much patience with these people who put nations into tidy parcels, who say the French are immoral, the Germans militaristic, the Jews money-lenders, the English arrogant and the Scots skinflints. The Welsh are usually put into two parcels. If they live in England and have made a bit of money selling milk and silk, Wales is the Land of Song and the Land of the White

Gloves[12], and the Welsh are the Salt of the Earth; but for those who stay at home because they love their country, we're a people with no backbone and a bunch of hypocrites. And yet, at the same time, there's a modicum of truth in all this, and from time to time the immorality and thirst for war and craving for money, the arrogance and meanness and hypocrisy, break out like pus from a boil on a man's head, and then it's everyone for himself.'

I knew there were answers to everything Wil said, but I couldn't for the life of me give them without feeling self-righteous and smug. The right answers aren't self-righteous or smug. According to psychologists, mental states are very different from the impressions that form them, and it follows naturally that there's a modification when mental states are turned into words. Is it, perhaps, blasphemous to think that's why a sheep falls silent before its shearers?

'Eat up, it's good for you,' Mam says. We are still one and the same to Mam. 'Eat,' she says, 'sleep, get up, don't, hurry up, be quiet...' all things which our legs and arms and eyes and ears can do. As far as she's concerned, we are flesh... flesh of her flesh.

We also cause her the same pain. Do you get enough food at Maes Mawr, Sionyn? Are there enough blankets on your bed? Be sure you've got enough warm clothes to wear. What sort of food do you get, Wil? Is it very cold in those old tents? Remember to wrap up warm, anyway. That old busybody Meri Owen Trycia was going on about Sionyn not being in the army. 'If everyone was like Sionyn,' I told her, 'there'd be no war.' 'Isn't it a pity Wil didn't make a stand like Sionyn,' said Mr Williams, the minister. 'We're very fortunate to have men like Wil,' I told him, 'or we'd all be trampled underfoot.'

Sometimes we don't know which of us is which. 'Do you remember, years ago, knocking Betsan Jones's door and then running away?' 'That wasn't me, that was you.' 'No it wasn't.' 'Yes it was, it was you.'

'Do you remember us two learning the catechism and Nain giving us a shilling each?' ''Course I do.'

'Which one of us fell out of the plum tree, then?' 'It was me,' I said. 'I'm absolutely certain of that.'

And so we come back to the plum tree. It's as inevitable as birth and death. As inevitable as the Day of Judgement, John

Huws Pant would say, and perhaps he's quite right. It's still there between the privy and the wall, older now and the green on its bark a little darker. One day Wil and I, I and Wil, climbed to the top of the plum tree. I perched on a branch that was withered like Nain's right arm and I fell and broke my leg. I had to stay in the house for weeks on end, with nothing to do except read and read and read. Wil made friends with Lias and little Harri from the garage, coming home every evening with talk of magneto and dynamo and clutch and changing gear and Blériot and Jerry M.[13] I couldn't care less about magnetos and dynamos and, to this day, Wil would rather be hanged than read a book.

Y Goeden Eirin (Gwasg Gee, 1946)

The Highest Cairn

The minister and the prisoner sat facing each other in the cell. If he had wished, the prisoner could have been as free as the minister. During the course of many years of daring and persistent crime, he had not been caught once. He had remained throughout a respectable, reasonably industrious member of society. He presided at eisteddfodau here, sat on committees there, played his part, went to conferences, dabbled in writing, and all with the same zeal and delight as he stole, deceived and tormented.

The successful conclusion of one villainy was the pleasurable beginning of the next. But when he walked into the police-station and said, I killed Lali Saunders, he thought, This is the end. There'll never be another chance. Lying and stealing and killing are all behind me now, as are the appetite and fine surfeit that follow in their wake; a slick murder and a grave for a whore. All that's left for me is a blindfold over my eyes, to step out of my cell, the monotonous chant of the prison chaplain, a rope, a sudden tug, the lime-pit, oblivion. This is the end. This was the fate the minister took to his bosom, an innocent victim that hurt and mutilated him, making him bleed.

'Are you a Welshman?'

'Yes, I am.' Welsh from Adam, a red-blooded Welshman, a Welshman through and through, a Welshman of long lineage, whatever expression is appropriate and acceptable to your prudish ears. There are other, coarser expressions, more sexual, literal ones. But in Welsh the daisy is observed without the sheep's droppings, the sleek skin of the horned cattle without their dung, the baby's curls and cooing without the bleeding womb.

> 'God is generous in His mercy
> Even to the worst of offenders.[1]

'God's mercy is inexhaustible, my boy... the thief on the cross... the eleventh hour... But one must repent... must repent... Do you repent?' He pleaded, he implored. Here is an opportunity for me to affirm my faith, to be given an assurance of Thy mercy; a chance to justify many long years of labouring in Thy vineyard. I have never been certain that I have saved a single soul. I have never had the satisfaction of knowing that I have led one poor lost wretch unto Thy paradise. I beseech Thee, O Lord, make me the vessel that brings this sinner under the shadow of Thy wing. Give me strength and guidance to demonstrate Thy pity and mercy, as we humbly submit and confess, I have sinned...

'God forgives and cleanses... not seven times, but seventy times seven...'[2]

An unending stream of rigmarole falling from his mouth like rotten teeth. His Adam's apple jerking inside his clerical collar, his Sunday face a holy yellow like a fasting man's, his voice imploring, beseeching, as if asking a favour. The prisoner looked at him, delighting in his naiveté. He grinned as he thought of the long years he had spent in the prison of his sanctity; years of scorching his big toes at the fire in his study, his hair growing grey as he pored over Biblical commentaries; trying to reconcile God's mercy with his justice, his love with his punishment; years of saying grace at table before spilling food down his waistcoat, and chewing, chewing, chewing like a cow and Gladstone[3]; years of standing in his polished pulpit on Sundays in front of fat people in fur coats and black coats and striped trousers; years when he had been blind to seven-in-a-bed poverty, disease, obscenities, passions, filth. A hopeless little creature, living in a fool's paradise, wretched in his ignorance, imploring, beseeching, begging. Give me something with which to justify my years. Remember the red robin on Thy threshold. Spare me a crumb... Well, you won't get any from me.

'I don't believe in God.'

'But my boy...'

He smiled when he saw the pain in the eyes of his prey, the excited flush in his cheeks, his pale lips. He got to his feet and turned his back. Tomorrow... . a sudden tug, the lime-pit. No communion for me, thank you very much... no more dainty morsels for me to chew over. I wonder whether Gwenallt[4] knows I'm here? Of course he does; the story was in the papers. I shall be saved by him, like the Jews at the expense of Jesus Christ. There'll be a short piece in *Yr Herald Cymraeg* on Monday... 'at W— Gaol... . has been hanged', and a brief paragraph in *Y Faner* and *Y Cymro*[5]...

'...though your sins be as scarlet, they shall be as white as snow... only repent...'[6]

'I never repented of anything in my life.' And that was true. He had never been sorry for anything... ever. He had never felt ashamed about his misdeeds, whether lies, deception, robbery, or murder. As far as he was concerned, they were part of a pattern of slick dishonesty, of skilful sins, of deliberate, conscious steps to self-destruction... feats in which one could take pride. As their creator, he could say of them all, 'And I saw that they were good.' For Francis of Assissi,[7] the joy of his poverty, for Wilberforce[8] his freed slaves, for Robert Owen[9] his clean factories, for Lewis Valentine[10] his baptism and prison; and for me, the lies: deception, violence, murder, all are mine. But Achilles[11] had his heel and Llew Llaw Gyffes[12] his tub and billy-goat, and his weak spot was a soft heart. He had never been able to look upon his actions and his victims as one. They were separate things, unconnected and taken apart, and while he took pride in the one he took pity on the other. Because for every deception there was a credulous innocent; for every clever robbery a sad loser; for every act of violence one who wept with shame, and for every murder a limp body and blood. On the one hand there was picking one's nose, scratching at a scab, shaming someone, stealing, living in sin, killing; on the other there was Mam, little Phil, Lisa Jones, Lali Saunders.

Don't pick your nose, Mam used to say. But later I made a fine art of picking it. I knew precisely when a snot was ready to be plucked out with a finger-nail. I would dislodge it in one fell swoop. And Oh, the lovely feel of rolling it into a ball between finger and thumb before disposing of it.

All right, Mam. I would run up to the bedroom, at the back of the house, somewhere out of the way, and stick my finger right up my nose.

Leave that snot alone, Mam would say.

But I knew the pleasure of anticipation and the delicious impatience before a scab becomes ripe. I would put my nail under it and feel its toughness and the sogginess of blood and pus, and decide that its time had not yet come. And when it did, I plucked it out tidily, and it would come off like a wart and I would run the tip of my finger along the smoothness of the new skin and see its fresh red colour.

All right, Mam. Smiling, I would look into her eyes and run into the garden, to Nain's house, anywhere out of her way, and scratch as much as I wanted.

'There is no sin so vile that God cannot forgive it, my boy... no sinner so base that God's grace cannot raise him up... only repent... only repent... You do believe that, don't you?' Give a blind man a penny! Give a blind man a penny!

Well, you won't get one from me!

'I don't believe in such nonsense... pure superstition.' The poor little spider under my foot. You have only your faith, a fragile basis for the things you are hoping for. Shield, helmet, sword... old-fashioned, romantic weapons from the age of legends. I have the great gun of my disbelief, Hurricanes, Waltzing Matildas...[13]

I remember my father saying, said Nain, how the creature at the police-station told his story. First he stole an apple – only an apple.

And then two apples, and three and four and five?

No, after that – money.

And then hundreds and hundreds of pounds?

No, sheep.

Sheep?

And the prisoner thought about the mysterious gradations of sin, the slithering from bad to worse, the slippery slope. But I wonder whether there are gradations to sin. I wonder whether stealing an apple is in essence just as much a sin as killing a man? What do you think, William Hughes?

The owner of the vineyard paid the same wages to the first worker as to the last.[14] I think, if the wages are the same, God metes out the same punishment for all sins.

Yes, well said. What say you, John Jones?

They were both paid a penny... the same as William Hughes.

The same as William Hughes... the same as Tomos. I shan't be able to read Rhys Lewis ever again, nor *Gwen Tomos* nor *Enoc Huws*[15]... never, never. I shan't be able to go to Sunday School ever again...

Are there gradations to sin?

Let's pull his trousers down, lads...

I wonder whether...?

We won't be long finding out.

And little Phil, too terrified to cry, held on to his braces, pleading with his eyes. This is shame's high-water mark... Jim afraid to go home after school because he'd been copying, Lewis crying because he had been caught out in a lie. Dora the Fron drowning herself before having her baby, Cain, Ananias, Saphira, Peter, Judas.[16] Draw closer to him cunningly, secure in his strength, corner him and scare him into limp obedience; show the patches on his shirt, the holes in his trousers, his birth-mark, his nakedness. Do it all craftily, in detail. To the actions of a coward were given the intensity and reverence of a religious rite. Don't cry, little Phil... don't cry. Look, I'll do up your trousers. Here, some marbles for you... and a top... and you can have my big hoop... Having silenced little Phil and seen him smile again, he noticed that little Phil's face ceased to be Phil's face at all. He took on the appearance of a boy... just a boy; not any particular boy, but the idea of a boy with a vacant, unfeeling, unrecognizable face. The action was everything now, and this boy nothing but a trivial necessity, a dead thing in his imagina-tion, a negative thing with no claim on his pity or sympathy, while he, on the other hand, was able to ponder contentedly, rejoice, laugh, swank in the skill of his attack.

A pound of sugar, please, Lisa Jones.

Anything else, dear?

No, nothing else, thanks. The old woman turns her back and he pinches an apple and puts it in his pocket.

Mam is asking if your rheumatism is better.

Yes, it is, dear, a lot better. Here's an apple for you. Thank you very much. He stuffs the apple into his pocket with the other and runs out of the shop.

Petty thefts, unconnected and pointless at first – things on their own like bachelors with no hope of becoming fathers. But gradually I found their progeny. For a bar of chocolate I could catch Alis the Pant at the rear of the chapel after the Fellowship meeting. Gravel crunching under our excited feet, the smell of lavatories, and a kiss.

And so on, from rung to rung, from rung to rung. Upwards?

Downwards? For me, up to the grey pinnacles, groping from their mist into the light shed by the security of accomplished mischief, and laughing at their crags and sharp ridges.

You won't ever leave me, will you?

No.

Will you marry me, perhaps?

Pr'aps.

You do love me, don't you?

Yes.

And everything will be all right with the child?

'Course.

She felt the artful power of his monosyllabic replies, so definite, unambiguous, inspiring confidence and trust.

I can sleep soundly now...

Yes...

Yes, you can sleep soundly, soundly, soundly. Hush a bye, baby... the boat is setting sail... hush a bye, baby... the captain is on board... Yes, the captain's on board. He had only to put out the gaslight then, and withdraw quietly, quietly. He opened the door and closed it fast behind him. Opening it again, he whispered, 'Good-night,' just to be sure. A half-mocking good-night, half jocular and self-satisfied.

Then he stepped into the convenient darkness to think over the poetic beauty of the act, the wealth of the details and their leisurely certainty. Here I am on the crest, having reached its strange light, turned my back on the ferny expanse of the lower slopes, strode across the marshland to the sustenance of green pastures... Has anyone new stayed behind tonight? asked William Hughes. Yes... yes... well, the silence says that no one has... Is there anything else to achieve? I ask. And the silence of the peak answers there is none. But here comes the minister to interrogate me: an anxious little creature, familiar with his Bible and Lewis Edwards, having read a bit of Plato and Kant, having played with the fire of Karl Marx and Nietzsche[17]; knowing enough not to be sure of anything. Killing your fellow-man is a serious matter. Killing faith is even worse. Yes, I'll come down to talk to you, to enquire about your experiences, to give you advice, to stuff the great truths down your throat, to make you a full member of the great brotherhood...

'God? Atonement? Forgiveness? What is God? The Atonement is an old wives' tale. Forgiveness in the imagination...'

'But my boy... my boy...' This is the test. Here in this cell, my God is being put to the test. If Thou art the Son of God... Who art Thou?... Art Thou the true vine, the bread of life... the good shepherd? Art Thou the only begotten Son that whoever...? Art Thou the Lamb of God who takest away the sins of the world? What am I? A bundle of sensations? The effects of environment and my forefathers? An ordained vessel for the whims of men? A slave to the secretion of my glands? He felt feeble, his virtue and energy draining from him. He bowed his head on the table and wept.

'Don't cry... don't cry... I was talking for the sake of talking...'

'Talking for the sake of talking?' He was startled, innocently swallowing the bait.

'All these have I kept from my youth up... .'[18]

'Yes, my boy... .'

'Father of mercy and the God of all consolation... .'

'Yes, my boy... .'

'He saves even in the worst instances... .'

'Yes, my boy... .'

''Tis mercy I am seeking and I shall seek it again...'[19]

'Blessed be the name of the Lord!' He fell to his knees. 'I thank Thee... thank... grace... great patience... mercy... pity... justice...' He wove the attributes into a paean of praise to the Lord for sending him back to his study fire, to grace at table, to his polished pulpit.

The prisoner had now forgotten everything about him as a man. He had ceased to be anything to him except a tool in an experiment – the greatest experiment of his life, a fitting end before oblivion. He had reached the summit of Snowdon.[20] He had stood on the top of the highest cairn. He had looked down on the lowlands between him and the sea and his mother; down at the galleries of the quarry and Little Phil and Lisa Jones; down at the Carneddau and Alis the Pant and all her kind; down on Lliwedd and the Aran and Lali Saunders.

Y Goeden Eirin (Gwasg Gee, 1946)

The Communion

Meurig Lewis and his companion stood in the narrow cleft that led to Dyffryn Ysig.[1] One more step and they would be cut off from the outside world and enclosed by the grassy pastures of Cwm Ysig's flanks on the one hand and by Cwm Igwl's on the other. The mountains spread their lower slopes like two brides to form between them a long strip of level land that had no waste, was tractable, and kind to man and beast. In the distance stood a farmhouse, smoke rising vertically from its chimneys in the silence of a breezeless afternoon.

'And this is Dyffryn Ysig?'

'Yes, this is Dyffryn Ysig.'

'Have you been here before?'

'Scores of times... with my father and mother. My father's an angler.'

The word 'father' went through Meurig like a knife. He had been an illegitimate child and had been brought up in a 'home'. He had never known who his parents were. He was, like the contemporary literature of Wales, pitifully ignorant of his lineage. He knew nothing of the virtues of his father or grandfather and so could not emulate them, nor of their faults so that he might avoid them. He had never felt the joy of being told that his eyes were blue like his mother's, nor that his forehead was high like his grandmother's.

He could remember the impersonal kindness of the Home Warden just as the contemporary writer remembers Ceiriog's[2] longing for the heather and the birds and the mountain. The kindness was as formal to the Warden as 'Nant y Mynydd' is to the schoolchildren of Wales, and as ineffective. He was no more able to muster up a connection and feel sympathy for his forefathers than schoolchildren in our vacuous culture can feel that hiraeth for the sea and great mountain is the same as Ceiriog's, that it was the same hiraeth made Pantycelyn[3] gaze across the distant hills and it is that old hiraeth which pushes its bedfellow closer and closer to the edge of the bed; that it was the same hiraeth made Branwen break her heart for her brother and Heledd weep in the dark hall of hers.[4]

Yesterday, Meurig had been jealous of his companion on account of his family, but here, from the moment he saw the valley, he felt some close, inexplicable relationship with everyone and everything, as if it had been born of the woods and had sucked the breasts of the river, and fattened on the sustenance of the lush pasture. He too had a father and mother.

He flung his pack aside and sat on the riverbank. His companion did the same.

'Dyffryn Ysig... Valley of the bruise...' he said to himself. He watched his companion toss a lock of fair, curly hair from his eyes. His hand was smooth and his fingers long and slender like a girl's. 'A bruised and afflicted heart,' he said aloud.

'O Ysig, you do not mock the afflicted objector,'[5] said his companion. There was an innocent look on his face, like that of a contented child, and his eyes were smiling. Meurig felt so close to him that he had to hurt him.

'Against her will, is it?'

He blushed as if Meurig had hit the mark, and the smile disappeared.

'What's your name?'

His companion picked up a stone and threw it into the river, and he heard his mother scolding in the sound of the splash.

'What's your name?'

'Gwyn.'

'Gwyn what?'

'Gwyn Morgan.'

He felt like a teacher questioning a small child on its first day at school. He nearly asked for the names of his mother and father, and where he lived.

'My name is Meurig Lewis.' Gwyn took no notice.

'There's Cefn Igwl,' he said, pointing to the farmhouse. Meurig shaded his eyes and gazed into the distance. At the far end of the valley he could make out a cluster of buildings. Above the two mountains rose six hundred feet or more from the valley bottom. There was a narrow gap between them... much narrower even than the cleft in which they were sitting. The rock-face there was much more rugged and the sides of the cleft bared their fangs like two great cross-cut saws with their teeth inter-locked. Near the top of Cwm Igwl, the distance masking the untidiness and jaggedness caused by the work of man, a pile of rubble stood out like a knuckle. He saw the white thread of the river near its source and could follow its leaps and bounds over rapids to the still waters of the lakes at the bottom along the four miles or more of its length, until it flowed deep and lazy at his feet, and the gravel on its bed as clear as moss and the grass of its banks. With several tributaries flowing into it, it looked like the spine of a giant fish. The whole scene served only to deepen Meurig's initial excitement. This was his home, and his father's and his mother's and his grandfather's and his grandmother's, and this was his small brother at his side.

'Is there anyone other than Ifan Davies and his wife living at Cefn Igwl?'

'Yes, Lowri.'

'Lowri?'

'Their daughter. She's a beauty.' Gwyn picked a reddish daisy and plucked its petals one by one and threw them into the river. 'Rolling ragged Lowri round the rugged ridge. Can you say that quickly?'[6] There was merry laughter in his eyes.

Meurig looked at him and felt old enough to be his father.

'What did you study at College?'

'Music.'

'The piano?'

'Yes, mostly... and the violin.'

'Do you play the piano well?'

'Yes, I do... quite well... ,' he answered simply, humbly.

'Farming won't do your hands any good.'

Gwyn spread his hands and looked at them. Meurig had never seen longer, stronger fingers. They were as flexible and slim as twigs. He flexed them like the Hamelin piper[7] yearning for an instrument.

'No, farming won't do them any good at all.' Tears welled in his eyes and trickled down his cheeks. He made no attempt to dry them, letting them be as if he were proud of them. A pang of pity raced through Meurig's body. He felt uncomfortably small. He would have to say something.

'I have no father or mother,' he said. His words sounded ridiculously disjointed. But what else could he have said? 'It's a great loss,' he added.

'Why?' There was no tremor in Gwyn's voice at all. It was perfectly clear, as if the tears on his cheeks were only drops of rain. Meurig's shame evaporated.

'You lose the sense of continuity... lose an inheritance.'

'The only inheritance worth having is the one you earn for yourself.' He spoke quickly, in a clipped, authoritative way. Now Meurig was the child. 'T.S. Eliot[8] says somewhere that tradition and a sense of continuity are not things to be inherited but to be learned by sweat and labour.'

'I'm not sure I understand.'

'I hope one day to be able to compose music of good quality. I know I have the ability, I was born with it. But what use is it if I don't study the works of the great composers down the centuries, and discover the excellence and shortcomings of each of them, and know what Beethoven learned from those who went before him, and what he in turn has to teach to those who come after? I have to learn how to distinguish between the good and the meretricious... and it's not a matter of taste, mark you... and be able to give reasons for my opinions. To see the past as a whole is to understand tradition, to see one age growing out of the other through admiration and emulation or loathing and reaction... one is as much a response as the other.'

He fell silent for a moment. Then, 'Losing a father and mother must be a loss to the emotions. But not to the intellect.' He got up, looked around him and the child-like expression came back into his eyes. 'You see that rowan tree over there?' he asked. 'I hid a penny at the base of its trunk about a month ago. I wonder if it's still there?'

For a moment Meurig followed him with his eyes. Then he turned his head and looked at the river, suddenly feeling alone. Not his old loneliness, but independence; nothing miserable, self-pitying and soft, but something strong, adventurous. He sensed, without knowing why, that it was something which arose from his environment and that his new companion was a strange amalgam of child and man, male and female. He had been on his own many times before. Tiring of the hubbub at the Home, he used to escape to the quiet of Nant Cae Ffridd, enjoying the muteness of the hazel-tree and the crooked oak-tree and the ash-tree and the black tracks of the woodpecker on their light-grey bark. Weary of the arguments among his fellow-lodgers in College Road over the orthography of Hebrew and the deity of Jesus Christ, and their arrogant self-confidence in analyzing the condition of their forefathers according to the theories of Adler and Freud,[9] and some of their own devising, he had often found relief watching the whirlpools under the Menai Bridge. And on the threshold of Dyffryn Ysig with its two mountains and farmhouse and pile of rubble and river and Gwyn, he suddenly felt a happiness unlike any other. He turned his back now on the noise and commotion of the world, on the lies in the newspapers, on the credulity of the common people, on the intolerance of the educated classes. He was in daily communion with the indifference of wood and water and plough and red earth, the understanding of horses and sheepdogs, the friendship of farm labourers and maidservants, whose only contact with the outside world was at season's end and the occasional Saturday in town. And he was at home.

He was delighted. It was not a vague idea in his head, not just a state of mind, ambiguous as the dusk, neither one thing nor the other like sleet, but something material, flesh and blood, quickening his heartbeat like a girl, warming his blood like a healthy appetite, consuming him from head to foot. He observed Dyffryn Ysig from one cleft to another, across its smooth blue bed and its wooded sides, and he beheld the kingdom of heaven. He turned the aftergrass and the new corn as work given him from the right hand of God. In the bubbling of the small brooks which lose themselves in the water of the Ysig he heard the Song of Moses and the Song of the Lamb. The trees clapped their hands and chanted to him as they dropped their myriad green leaves. The Son of Man walked upon the stone walls and intensified the colours of the flowers and quickened the wings of robin and wren. He was at home. He breathed easily the thin clear air of the heavenly places. He felt neither fear nor terror, no surprise and no admiration even. From the moment his inheritance was announced to him he saw and smelt and heard and tasted and felt himself to be a natural, comfortable citizen of the world which had been granted unto him. Here was none of the sanctimony he had experienced in chapel, none of the woolly excess of sentiment which had brought a lump to his throat once or twice during prayer-meetings at the Students' Christian Union, none of the spirit of resolution-making which had enraptured him in the last service of the Caernarfon Session. Indeed, he felt no conventional religious or moral or godly appeal. It was not the Bible he had read from that moment on, but *Cit* and back-numbers of *Cymru'r Plant* and *Sioned*.[10] The birds of the air sang of the Malltraeth Cob and the Fleece of the Yellow Sheep. And he felt almost suffocated with happiness that, for him, the Son of Man had walked the hills of Wales, and not those of any other country under the sun. The joy of the ages was his.

I want to call our sheepdog Seth, Tomos Bartley.[11]

Do you, brother Roli?

You have as much regard for Seth as Twm has for me, haven't you?

To be sure.

The sadness and despair of centuries were intermingled.

And are you disappointed, Saunders Lewis?[12]

Yes, Morus Kyffin[13]... they are hypocrites... and they deny their language and their God.

How long, O Lord... how long?

A chair was placed for him on the hearth with as little fuss and ostentation as when Siôn Jones Talgoed was received into the Fellowship at Seion.

'We are very glad to see Siôn Jones calling to see us at last,' said the minister. 'Is there some verse or a word of experience...?'

'You get on with your work,' said old Siôn, 'and don't take no notice of me. I made a bit of a mistake... a bit of a mistake, that's all. I thought there was an Election meeting going on here... An Election meeting. But I like it well enough here... like it well enough... delighted, really.... Go on, Mr Williams... and thank you very much...'

Old Siôn brought Meurig back to earth. He saw Cwm Ysig and Cwm Igwl and the grassland between them and the sullen river and the farmhouse as they had been before they were purified in the fire of experience. And there was not that much difference between them; yet never again would they put on immortality and shine with the inner light. The first excitement had died away, it's true, but there was still some constant, abiding warmth.

He had not felt a whit better. He was unable to promise himself that he would never have lewd thoughts again. He would still enjoy farting and would continue to take God's name in vain. He knew that in his constitution there would still be that thing which allowed him to enjoy a bawdy story and gossip. He knew it was not impossible that he would one day be excluded from the Fellowship.[14] But he also knew it would not be out of need that he would commit any of his old sins from now on. They were natural tendencies that arose inevitably from the body, soul and spirit which made up his individual self. He was not a whit more certain of any credo or philosophy. Doubting the existence of God had always been for him an affectation, yet he was very unsure of what it was. All the goodness of the world sometimes: the accumulation of centuries of good deeds, everyone sucking like leeches the marrow of the past, and turning in the fullness of time into skeletons for their children to fatten on. And God had always existed because all these things had always been possible. The Atonement and Mediation were only words, and although they helped you get into the kingdom of heaven, they were still only words as far as he was concerned. For years he had been absolutely convinced that his love for his country was a good and manly thing, and not narrowness or the cause of war. This certainty had continued.

And yet, although he realized that no essential changes had happened to him, he did not feel altogether certain. Abstract expressions like humility, sympathy and tolerance slipped into his mind. They were ambiguous, vague, shapeless as pebbles on the bed of a rushing river. Humble to whom? Sympathy with whom? Tolerate what and why?

At his feet grew a clump of groundnuts and on their tough tops there were greyish-white flowers, as big as a child's open palm. He took out his pocket-knife and cut around the stem of one. He dug until he could feel the tip of his finger under the nut and pulled it out carefully by its root. He cleaned it and enjoyed its dry brittleness between his teeth and the taste of earth on his tongue. He knelt down, his head hanging over the river-bank, and drank the water in many draughts.

'Drink this... for this is my...'[15]

Springing to his feet, he trembled with the boldness of his

imagination. But soon the fear subsided and left behind it a peaceful feeling of inevitable and eternal union between the green earth, soil and water. He had come into his inheritance.

Y Goeden Eirin (Gwasg Gee, 1946)

On the Mend

Glyn had been taken straight from the boat that rescued him in... to a mental hospital in North Wales. He was sitting there now in an armchair in a comfortable room. At his side, holding a bowl of bread-and-milk, stood a nurse, her apron white as communion linen.

'Here's the mouse lobscouse. I've put four mule hooves in it. Not the mule in the cellar but the one in the cowshed eating linseed porridge.'

'Where are the shoeing tongs?'

'Here they are.' She gave him a spoon.

'Dog and cat and cat and dog,' he chanted.

'And me and him and him and me.' Sali finished the couplet and they both shook with laughter.[1]

Sali sat like a tailor at his feet. She held her breath until her cheeks were swollen like the crusts of two loaves. Her eyes bulged in her head like those of a fish. She pummelled her cheeks with her fists and made a noise like a threshing-machine.

'Boo! Boo! Boo!' she said.

Glyn had never heard anything more beautiful in his life. He thought how lovely it would be to sit like this for ever and ever. The scream of a pig being ringed is pretty, and the cries of a man with his fingers in the threshing machine, but nothing quite as good as this.

And in thinking of pigs and a threshing machine, he thought of muck and the stench of dungheaps and cowsheds not cleaned out, and leeches sucking blood, and his whole body was filled with an exceedingly great happiness. It pulsed in streams through his veins and spilt over in uncontrollable, fierce laughter.

Glyn had never been healthier. His whole body was so light he felt as if he had no body at all. There was never a nasty taste on his tongue, he never had a headache, nor ever felt sick; and the most exciting thoughts flashed through his mind to turn his life into an adventure story. The horned sheep became a coat of many colours to warm Morus the Wind.[2] For long intervals he was king of Caer Arianrhod,[3] and the Foel and the Cilgwyn and the little Dolydd river paid tribute to him; and once he saw

Alexander the Great[4] with his arm around the neck of old Beti Ty Mwd. Time did not exist, nor distance. He strode from continent to continent as smoothly and without hindrance as the Sleeping Bard.[5]

'The darling of my heart... ,' sang someone outside.

'Shut your gob, you ugly sod...'

'They were preachers, almost every one, on their way home of a Monday morning...'[6]

'I want to go home! Can I go home? Mam! Dad! Can I go home?' And someone was weeping to break your heart.

And this was his heaven's gate. There wasn't much satisfaction in singing and shouting and swearing and reciting. They were like a good tune melting into itself, starting off as tremendous fun and dying away like a lullaby. The noise outside and the bowl of bread-and-milk and linseed porridge and the nurse pummelling her cheeks changed into a rainbow on the ceiling. Their colours ran into one another. He could not see where one began and the other ended. Enchanted, he lay down on the floor, staring and staring. He felt perfectly content, happy, unworried, with health and vigour and strength plucking at his fingertips and leaping to his toes.

Sali got up and took the empty bowl.

'Monkey on a stick and a bear in the loaf,' she said.

'And four calves scolding the Menai Bridge,' he replied, laughing and laughing fit to split his sides. He leapt up to follow Sali into the next ward. He stood at a table where two patients were chatting over their breakfast.

'"There's something wrong with your stomach," he said to me. "My stomach, doctor?" I said, "but it's my big toe that's hurting."'

'It's quite true there'd be no Doctrine of Atonement without Lewis Edwards, but there'd be no Lewis Edwards without the Doctrine of Atonement, either.'

'Clever people,' said Glyn to himself. He fetched a chair and sat down near them. He sensed sanctuary there and university learning. The sound of the two sipping their tea from their saucers and devouring their sandwiches was like a blessing, their warm breath like incense.

Sali tickled the nape of his neck and he chased her into his

own room. She took paper and pencil from a drawer and gave
them to him.

'Cat,'[7] she said. And laboriously, with his tongue sticking out
like a schoolboy's, he wrote 'tac'. She smiled at him. 'Tea,' she
said. He wrote 'aet', and held it out at arm's length to admire it.
He was convulsed by his success, giddy with happiness. It made
his eyes shine and put colour in his cheeks. It put a lovely rest-
lessness in his fists and strength in his legs.

'Mam,' said Sali, without changing the tone of her voice.
'Mam,' he wrote. Something like a wild bird streaked through his
mind, and in an instant of anguish he became aware of everything. Naked and clear like plain truth. Pale and quiet, he threw
away his pencil.

Sali seized the first chance in weeks. 'Your mother's coming
to see you today.'

But it was too late. Glyn had not heard anything so funny for
a long while. The sound of the words was exactly like the Little
Black Cobbler breaking wind atop the White Stile.[8] A flood of
laughter surged within him. It broke through the dam of his
mouth in an uncontrollable, destructive stream. Sali bit her lip to
keep back her tears, and laughed and laughed with him.

Surreptitiously, Glyn gave her the slip. He rushed through the
tansy beds. He kicked the flowers' heads in every direction and
snapped the lusty buds of the roses. He took pleasure in his
flowing blood, in the open wounds, the gore that had collected in
them.

Not far away two men in shirt sleeves were working at a
steaming dungheap. One spat at him and the other flung a
forkful of manure at him. He leapt into the midst of the heap.
The filthy quag seeped through the soles of his boots, the moss
giving quietly under his weight. He put his hands into it and ran
them through his fair hair. He was beside himself with pleasure.

His mother arrived the minute Sali finished washing and
tidying him. An old woman dressed in a black coat and black hat
with a bit of white in the ribbon and, in her blouse, a brooch
made out of a gold sovereign. Glyn was the youngest of her six
children. He took no notice of her greeting and grasped her hand
in a surly fashion as he shook it.

'Feeling better, my boy?'

He snarled at her. 'Boo! Boo!' he said, as children do when they pretend to frighten each other.

'I've brought you some eggs... and a little butter...'

'Boo! Boo!'

Tears welled in her eyes and trickled down her cheeks, forming an irregular mark. Glyn could not take his eyes off them. He stared, enchanted by their zigzag course through her wrinkles. They were Sue and Mue running a race. Sue's winning. No, Mue. No, Sue.[9]

'Sue, Mue... Sue, Mue...'

He put his hand under his mother's chin and two tears dropped into it and lay intact, like quicksilver, on his dry palm. He licked them like a cat and held out his hand for more.

'I think it's best if you go, Mrs Evans,' said Sali.

'Yes, isn't it?' The old woman got to her feet and went out immediately.

A few days later Glyn woke up with an icepack on his head, heat sores on his lips and fatigue and listlessness in all his limbs. His mouth was on fire and his tongue felt like risen, baked dough in it. He could neither open his eyes nor put his hand to his forehead to ease the tick-tock, tick-tock of the pain there. He heard a voice far off.

'This may bring him to his senses. A high temperature does that sometimes.'

It was as if someone was writing the words on his brain with the point of a pocket-knife. He trembled with gladness. From head to toe he felt shivers of rejoicing and everything fell into place. Bread-and-milk was bread-and-milk. The horned sheep grazed once again under its weight of wool on the river's bank. Joseph[10] wore his coat of many colours. Caer Arianrhod sank under the sea at Dinas Dinlle and the Foel and the Cilgwyn raised their shoulders behind Bryn Gorwel as proudly and as sturdily as ever. The little Dolydd river wandered through the fields between its rushy banks without a red penny of debt to anyone and something came into his mother's apron and the pitcher was back on her head on the White Stile.

He felt that he wanted to live his life over again... to remember everything that had ever happened to him, everything he had seen and heard; to gather it all for a moment into the same place like a multicoloured marble; to charm it into his mind and set it on and give it a shove as the farmer rounds up all his cattle in the yard on the day of the auction.

He gave himself up body and soul to his memories. They paraded before him like a cloud of witnesses. He remembered a warm bed, and the cat with its kittens lying across its mouth, a line on a Monday morning full of underclothes blowing in the wind like corpulent men, the white and purple flowers of the potato patch, the sparks that flew from his new clogs. He remembered a cake soggy with blackberries and sweat steaming off the back of the Llwyn Piod mare.

He remembered the spring in Nant Cae Ffridd and the sticky buds bursting like sores and healing into pretty green leaves, the grey anemone like tubercolosis with its black and green serrations, the clumps of primroses, their fragrance drifting like an echo, a lonely daffodil illuminating the shade at the foot of a tree, the yellow flag and blue iris like thick-legged louts in the dampness, the Pant Rhedyn cattle straying and chewing the cud in the rushes, the water-wheel in the distance creaking on its axle.

He remembered Wili Bach Taldrwst, his face like chalk after smoking coltsfoot; Ianto Cae Doctor unable to lift his rheumatic leg over the crossbar of his bike; Mag Cae Glas cursing her brother under her breath; Lisi Storws running to hide because she was ashamed of her baby. And he remembered Robin Ty Tân legless in town of a Saturday night, his breath smelling like a brewery, pressing sixpence into his hand, 'Here, by dam... for your mother's sake... the finest old thing in the world... yes, dammit all...'

'Thank you, O Lord,' he said to himself like old Robat Tomas Cim in his disjointed prayers, 'for health in mind and body... our time went by yesterday, our time today is...'

And he had today, a blessed possession, overflowing with happiness. Yesterday with its sadness and grief and pain and suffering had passed. The sun had risen on today, the first day of his rebirth; today was full of riches and rejoicing, promising bliss and living strength and sustenance for his body and soul.

'... there is no tomorrow for anyone... save for those who seek God...'

Something cracked in his head. It was like a gunshot. The

cows scattered from his mind's yard, leaving nothing behind but the echo, and that echo was followed by another and another and another. Instead of dying away they reinforced each other until in the end they swelled into a coarse and brutish neighing. And the neighing put on flesh and he saw a white mare and after it a red mare and a black mare and a pale grey mare.[11]

His mouth and throat were on fire.

'A drink of water.' His own voice frightened him. It sounded like the voice of someone he had known as a child. Sali was at his side in an instant. She put a wet feather to his lips.

'Are you better?' Her voice quavered as she spoke.

He opened his eyes. 'How long have I been here?'

'Very nearly a year.'

'Does Mam know?'

'Yes.'

A cloud passed across the sun and a sudden squall of wind with rain in it disturbed the curtains at the window.

'A thousand times more beautiful is the fair one...'[12]

'Shut up, you dirty old bitch...'

'Not charity for a man but work... a man is too great for charity...'[13]

'I want to go home! Can I go home? Mam! Dad!'

The neighing stopped and the horses disappeared, leaving only a dull pain behind.

'Is the war still on?'

'Yes.'

'All the pain and suffering... suffering and pain... pain and suffering...'

'Don't upset yourself. You must get really better now... you're on the mend.' She settled the pillow for him and wiped the perspiration from his brow.

'Was I happy while I was...?'

'Yes, you were, happy as a lark... laughing all the time... laughing and laughing...'

'Laughing and laughing...' He was quiet for an instant. 'Pity I'm on the mend.'

'Oh, don't say that.'

'Yes it is, an awful pity...'

Y Goeden Eirin (Gwasg Gee, 1946)

The Stepping Stones

'I've written a story,' said Absalom[1] to Tomos and Enid.[2]

'Have you, indeed?' said Tomos in his patronising way, ready for anything.

'I hope it's got a proper plot,' said Enid. 'I'm fed up with these stories without a structure, that presuppose an idea and Freudian analysis are sufficient to create literature.'

Absalom and Enid do not agree about what makes a plot. Enid has an imagination that sees things happening to people's bodies. She can see a man and wife sitting in a garden of a summer evening and the girl next door, with a single word and seemingly innocent smile, causing a rift between them. She can imagine the thieves in their cave and Don Pedro sticking his knife into Donna Theresa's bosom.[3] She sees people drinking and eating, writing letters, marrying, sleeping, dying. But what Absalom sees are people living, moving and being inside themselves, and if they happen to write a letter or marry or fall asleep or die, they do so out of convenience for him, not out of any inner motivation.

'You don't create living, moving characters, people doing this and that in particular places at specific times for specific purposes, with credible actions following naturally one after the other in chronological order,' said Enid, 'people whom the likes of me can imagine and believe in and understand. What you write about is some prematurely born offspring which, for want of creative imagination, you can mould and dissect according to your own whim, mixing its past and present and future into one incomprehensible mess.'

'I don't mind if you want to put it like that,' Absalom said. 'I don't see why I have to devise credible circumstances. What's important is to see that the characters' response to their circumstances, whether credible or not, is a true, full, fair one. If Ariander Peregrin is on the summit of Everest five minutes before dawn on the last Christmas Day of the world, it is to ensure that Ariander's response to his particular circumstance is a correct, fair, credible, significant one.'

'The truth is,' said Enid, 'you can't write a simple, straightfoward story. Affected pseudo-philosophising – that's what your stories are. Your characters don't marry; they interrogate themselves about whether they should marry; it's not enough for them to be fathers and mothers, they burrow into the depths of their subconscious trying to discover what complicated, concealed, perverse motives made them sleep with one another in the first place...'

'Are motives needed for something like that?' said Tomos.

They ignored him.

'... and in realizing them, in order to save face, try to rationalize them. Absalom, I wouldn't want to hurt or discourage you... but...'

'My dear Enid, you won't hurt or discourage me. For better or worse, nobody's opinion, for or against, has any effect on me. Whether my stories meet with praise or disapproval, I am neither heartened nor disheartened. It was not always thus. There was a time when a forthright opinion, Yes or No, was necessary to me, and the indifference of a lukewarm Yes-and-No gnawed at me like hunger. That's why, when I was seventeen, I decided to die.'

'Die?'

'Yes, die. To me at that time to die seemed... to die romantically, disastrously... the only way to corner my mother and get her to express her exact feelings towards me.'

'I don't understand.'

Mam was a laodicean woman. I never learned from her what precisely her feelings for me were, how exactly she thought of me.

Mam, I was first in my class this time. I beat Tomos and Elwyn and Arthur...

Were you? Listless, cold.

Mam, I told Mr Davies, the minister, to mind his own bloody business.

Did you? Listless, cold.

Mam, I've won the chair at the Urdd Eisteddfod[4] this year.

Have you? Flat, distant.

Mam, I've... I've decided not to take communion any more.

Have you? Flat, distant.

I did not believe in the idea of a mother. A woman, just because a particular process has taken place inside her over a specific period, does not inevitably become at the end of that period kind, unfailingly tender, naturally self-sacrifing. I had no belief (I still haven't) in some inexhaustible supply of motherhood that is kept somewhere, and that a woman, when her child is born, in the capacity of a mother, drinks of it her share of mercy and pity, patience and love, slowness to wrath, and forgiveness. Don't misunderstand me. I'm not saying there aren't kind mothers. Of course there are. But there are the other kind too. There are mothers who treat their children as banks or an insurance policy. There are mothers who delight in sacrificing their children, in an abstract way, for a king they have never seen; there are mothers who suffocate their children with excess of love. Mothers aren't bodies possessed of unchanging virtues, but individuals and qualities and faults all different from one another and mixed in as wide a variety as there are mothers in the world. Jane Hughes is the mother of Tomos. Ann Williams is the mother of Arthur, but Susan Price, a former Mathematics teacher at the Tre-fôn County School, is my mother. All three have the instinct to take care of us just as Siwsi, the cat, has an instinct to look after her kittens.

It may be that these ideas are completely wrong. Perhaps they violate all the rules of logic. But remember, the effect of believing them, whether true or false, was not one whit the less. Their correctness or their incorrectness or their infantile platitude did not lessen my anguish one bit. For you, I was an ignorant innocent, but for me, I was a prey to consuming curiosity to know about the mind and feeling of the woman who in the fullness of time had given me birth.

I was as familiar with her physical appearance as with the palm of my own hand: her hair, her forehead, her ears, her nose, her eyes, her lips, her teeth, her throat. I remember the blemish when she lost a hair from her eyelash, and my fear lest the fine feathers under her nose should turn into a disfiguring moustache. I watched the white marks on her nails reaching to her fingertips.

You're coming into money, Mam... white marks on your nails...

Am I?

But it was only a familiarity with her body. I was never able to rend the veil of her indifference. As a lad I liked to think it was only something that had been acquired, some sort of defensive shield to save me from fears of which I knew nothing. I tried to imagine what yearnings and thoughts and tendencies were behind the mask; what her preferences and attitudes were, her favourite things and what she disliked most. She was not without her notion of religion and politics and the arts. I insisted on her sitting with me at the fireside and talking... I have no difficulty in believing in the miraculous birth and the resurrection of Christ... what matter whether he was born miraculously or not, he said, 'Love one another', and that's enough... religion and politics are totally separate things, one doesn't have to limit the other... it's a man's religion that decides his politics; there is no difference between them in essence, they are one...; poetry must have a wide appeal, it's not something for the chosen few... if a poet's experience is sometimes obscure and over-personal, who can blame him if his expression of it is difficult, complicated...?

But instead of a definite opinion about anything, there was this terrible lack of interest. I became a moth; I was persistent.

Mam, a boy's best friend is his mother, isn't she?

Is she?

Mam, Tomos's mother tickles the soles of his feet and teases him about Cit Tyddyn Isa'.

Does she?

Mam, it was a nasty shock for Mary when she lost Jesus Christ on his way from Jerusalem, wasn't it?

Was it?

There was no chance of making a hole the size of a blackhead in the hard oak of her. Sometimes I would try a sharp attack.

Mam, you are my mother, aren't you?

Who else?

Mam, I do love you, love you, love you...

Not even a sharp intake of breath to betray the slightest prick of pain.

Oh Mam... come on, rebuke me or love me, one or the other... Oh Mam... give me a kiss, box my ears... Oh Mam, put your hands around my neck; smack my bottom; say, My pretty little darling; call me the little cub that breaks his mother's heart; spit on clay and open my eyes; smile at me and run your hand through my hair; tell people, Whatever he tells you to do, do it[5], and I shall be your dear son in whom you shall be well pleased. Oh Mam, cast me into the fiery furnace; ask what you will of me; shout My son, my son, why has thou forsaken me? And I shall be purified like the beautiful legion of martyrs.

I was at the time preparing for a scholarship to University. Our teachers spoke to us as if we were adults. Men, said the English teacher, men who are excited by deep, serious emotion are unable to say anything. They become a mute lump of feeling, a sensitive body of red-hot fire. For a moment their powers of expression die; they have control over only the most elemetanry words, the simple words of their childhood which are almost as independent of their minds and breath as the pulses of their heart. That is perhaps why Wordsworth[6] was not prompted to write his poetry during the first flush of emotion and why it was in the tranquility of a quiet hour long afterwards that his feeling crystalized into conscious, disciplined expression. Shakespeare knew this: 'Give sorrow words,' he wrote. 'The grief that does not speak whispers the o'erfraught heart and bids it break.'[7]

And I believed the whole lot. I doted on the theory, and suddenly one night, in my bed, the means of my deliverance became clear to me. I had to die. I must prepare for myself a death that would, by its wretchedness and disaster, overcome this dreadful muteness. An experienced hunter, I would pursue my mother to the glade in the wood and set my dogs on her. Their prickly tongues would slaver and she would turn to face them, all fear and sadness stilled in her eyes. No more indifference, no lack of interest any more, but in their place the anguished exclamations and restricted vocabulary of the sad in heart.

I knew nothing then of Logic; I hadn't heard of the premises and errors which cause illogicality; but looking back, I realize that, in my own way, I was reasoning myself into the grave, like a philosopher at his task. I said: no human being who feels something to the quick can express his experience; he falls mute; Mam is a human being; therefore, in the face of deep experience Mam will remain mute.

My purpose in life was now to discover the most effective way of forcing her to this depth of feeling. I read constantly; read and read and read; and my only aim at first was to identify various ways of dying. My death would have to be a mixture of the romantic and the tragic, both pretty and ugly, something in the tradition of Romeo and yet suggestive of the maggots that would long fatten on my skeleton, uniting the purity of Branwen's[8] despair on the Alaw's bank and the unsightly scars of Gwern, her son, amid the flames. I read about the Mayor of Cork[9] starving himself to death. I too could refuse food; each day I would grow a little thinner and turn grey and wither; my face would wear the other-worldly pallor of the recluse, and at last I would disappear like the moon at month's end and leave my mother in the darkness of her night. But this way had its disadavantages; perhaps my mother would grow hardened towards my stubbornness, or perhaps, since my death would be a very slow process, my mother would grow used to the idea of losing me and thus deprive my death of the necessary shock. I read about Shelley's body being burnt on the beach at Spezzia and his friend Trelawney leaping into the bonfire to save his heart.[10] I wept as I imagined my mother clasping my heart to her bosom. Or I would drown myself. I was fascinated by the limp helplessness of a drowned man. But one day I heard Shôs next door talking about Lias Tan Lan when he drowned at Dinas Nantlle. 'You never saw anything like it. He was blue-black, his eyes like red patches, his belly gleaming and blown up as if he was about to burst. It was the most sickening sight I've seen in all my born days.' There was no romance in a horrible thing like that.

I read Chekhov's *The Seagull*[11] and fully understood the despair and disappointment of Constantine. There was only one way out of my pain, as there was for him. I dreamt of the anguish of his desire for the approval of his mother. I took hold of the same gun... and held it to my temple...

These deaths were my stepping stones. From stone to stone I stepped closer to the greenness of the river's other bank to throw myself at last into mossy comfort, content with the sound of bees and drowsy in the scents of the hay-harvest. I liked the sturdiness of the stones, their reliability. There was moss and lichen on some of them, it's true, and the river sometimes made them smooth and dangerous so that my feet slithered from the dead rock into the living waters. But from the outset I had not eyes for the things around me. So great was my desire to reach the other side I was unaware of the smooth liveliness of the river between two stones, and its sudden whirlpools and foam, and its tossing and turning between mossy roots. I didn't see the trout making a perfect circle as they surfaced, nor the moorhen and its chicks, at a strange sound, suddenly ducking headfirst into the safety of a pool. A wagtail flashed past me unnoticed and just before it started raining the swallows caught their flies without my noticing them. I didn't see the sun on the water in the willow's shade, and the wood was quiet in wind and rain. I knew only the stones. I was familiar with every dent and bump in them, but the life around them, the living waters, the birds of prey and sun on water between the branches were completely dead to me.

Even so, I was not, like Keats,[12] half in love with easeful death. I did not choose it for its own sake. It was only a means of achieving my aim, and one death was only something to be compared with another, something to be weighed and measured and examined according to its effect. And thus, little by little, in studying it I acquired taste. My feeling receded a little; it was my mind would take action. I tried to make phrases that were scientific, unambiguous, deprived of any imaginary overtones, to explain to myself why I accepted one death and rejected another, just as a critic weans himself of his personal prejudices and preconceptions in evaluating a piece of literature. I made myself an expert in the fine art of dying. It was something that appealed mainly to my intellect, my feeling taking its proper place as one element among many. I set the solo of my intellect to the accompaniment of my feeling.

I don't quite remember when I first slipped into the water and chose the hard and transient happiness of the living rather than a barren grave. At first I wet my feet a little and glimpsed the great love of the Mayor of Cork for his country and the splendour of his intransigence and the bliss and excitement of his numbered days and the death that was only the logical conclusion to following Christ's example. I then began to slip more and more often and found myself sometimes going along with the current from Harlech and across the river Llinon,[13] standing at the ford in Annwn,[14] a goldsmith in Haverfordwest; sometimes struggling against the current and seeing blood on my hands that all the perfumes of Arabia would not wash away, sometimes plumbing the depths and seeing the creation moving in them, while dead in the grave.

And somehow, whatever its essence, whether the hiraeth of the son of the mountain for the birds and heather, or promises of Ynys Afallon,[15] or the terror that frightened the wild dove,[16] or Mr Jones the Parson pacing up and down his church during a carol service, or melancholy. My friends going home or the confidence of virtue... the same was its effect on me. I was inspired by sadness as much as happiness, as purified by sin as by virtue.

Many things wearied me. I couldn't understand how an artist of any sensitivity could conspire to kill his fellow-man. Should he not be full of the holy irresponsibility that casts reason and the everyday things and wisdom of this world to the four winds? Given that we cannot live a lifetime on the peaks, should not remembrance of the thin air enliven the dullness of the middle years? I wondered whether I should one day grow out of my superficial awareness of the external attractions of Nature, the clouds and rain, the hedges and the simple beauty of the life of the Aberdyfi Shepherd to feel the mystical excitements that make Menna 'Rhen and the Red Plough and the sound of the psalter and harp and the dear distant hills nothing more than symbols? Would I leap into the vacancy between Islwyn and Ceiriog?[17] And a thousand and one other things, until the magic stones lost their certainty and became nothing more than a part of the river and everything around them; slowing the current sometimes and catching a green leaf that swirled at their base, and imprisoning another in the clutches of those mossy fingers that brought autumn before its time. But sooner or later every leaf, whether slipping quietly between them or being victoriously driven over them when they are washed by the rush of the tempest.

I shall never forget my shock on first realizing this. I had by now done three years at College.

Mam, I want to withdraw my membership of Hebron...

Do you?

Sometimes as a lad I used to wake in the dead of night, and in the darkness have the terrible thought that both my eyes were running. I gazed and gazed without seeing anything. Like a madman I would leap out of bed and feel my way to the window. I would throw open the curtains and press my face against the pane... Jesus Christ, please don't let me go blind, I can't live if I'm to be blind, I'll say my prayers every night from now on, I'll try my best not to think about Lena Cae Glas before falling asleep... Gradually came the relief of making out two colours in the sky, and presently a clear light in the bedroom of little Ifan Ty'n Pistyll. That was the only panic I felt when I realized that my mother's indifference no longer had any effect on me. I felt as if I had lost something and in my initial terror I stumbled in my confusion to discover what intellectual endowments I had lost. But soon I saw smoke rising from the chimney of an empty house at Rhyd Ddu[18] and heard the sound of the old river Prysor singing in the cwm.[19]

I nurtured independence, not the arrogant independence that turns up its nose at approval and chastisement, for I am still glad when I am appreciated, and I grow sad when rebuked, but the gladness is no longer tinged with self-doubt and there is no indignation in the sadness. I now have a proper idea of what I am and a blessed sense of proportion. I opened the door of my claustrophic bedroom, my excessive interest in myself, to live in the broad halls of other people's experiences.

Absalom looked at Tomos and Enid.

'Well?' he said.

'My son, my son,' said Tomos. 'It's hard to say...'

'It's quite easy to say,' said Enid. 'Here, in a few words, is my idea...'

Y Goedin Eirin (Gwasg Gee, 1946)

Meurig

Thomas Lewis, Meurig's father, had at first intended to become a preacher, but the August Examination put a stop to that, and since handling tweed and underclothes was much cleaner and lighter work, and closer to his original ideal than handling slates, he chose to be apprenticed behind a counter rather than at the quarry.

He had gone on to marry his boss's daughter and buy a gold watch and chain. The courage shown in his youth, the responsibility of having a substantial sum in the bank and more than anyone else in the accounts of Seilo, the Calvinistic Methodist chapel in Llanifor, together with his prematurely greying hair, gave him the countenance of one of his denomination's Apostles of Peace. Because of the way he looked and the debts many of his fellow members owed him, he had been elected to the diaconate. He could not avoid the County Council after that, and unless something serious happened such as the centralization of authority, which would have deprived the people of the privilege of putting their cross against the names of shopkeepers and farmers and rich builders, thus sending them to Caernarfon to sit on committees and drink tea and promote their own businesses three or four times a week, he had every chance of becoming an Alderman in due course.

Meurig's mother had died when his sister was born and his Aunt Sal, his father's sister, had come to keep house for them and bring up the child. She behaved as if her brother had passed the August Examination. She had taught Meurig how important it was to say please and thank-you, not to dirty the tablecloth, to raise his cap to the daughters of The Laurels, and to sit as far away as possible from the other schoolchildren lest he caught fleas or something worse. She combed his hair every night with a fine-tooth comb. Once her efforts met with success. She had caught one of the something worse, and Meurig could still remember hearing the crackle of the corpulent little creature between her nails. But Meurig had been nearly twelve when his aunt moved in with them and could not forget that he had seen his mother weeping more than once alone in the bedroom, and

heard her saying, 'You're a hypocrite! I pray every night the boy
will grow up to be very different from you.' He did his best to
answer his mother's prayers.

Simple, superficial things at first. His father's voice was soft
as velvet, like a muted fiddle; so Meurig put on a high, raucous
voice. His father wiped his feet carefully before coming into the
house; Meurig entered the kitchen with his muddy shoes, despite
his aunt's scolding. His father would talk all day as long as there
was someone to listen, so Meurig kept his mouth shut for hours
on end. 'Sulking,' his aunt would say. 'A common little boy.'

As he grew older and began to perceive something of his
father's character, rather than just his physical appearance, he
stopped dwelling on the superficial differences and concentrated
on the mental ones. He discovered the true meaning of
'hypocrite'. When he first heard that word, it was synonymous
with King John and Crippen.[1] Many a night he lay awake for
hours, his eyes on the door, expecting to see his father enter in
with a sharp knife glinting in the moonlight. Later he realized
that a hypocrite was something that lost its broad smile in the
passage between the shop and parlour, something he and his
sister wore well, sumptuously even, to go to school and chapel
and for which they were reproached at home. Whenever his
father got up in chapel and said, 'My dear brothers and sisters,'
what he meant was, 'You money-owing rascals.' He made up
some true prayers for his father. 'Thank you for being so good
to my business. Let me learn whether the Black Mountain
Tobacco Company or the Gwaelod-y-Glyn Oatbread Company
is the better place to invest my money. Thank you for the inven-
tor of the secret ballot that prevents William Hughes of Ceiros
finding out that I didn't vote for his son.'

For this reason Meurig decided he would pay due respect to
God, believe in him wholeheartedly and worship him sincerely.
The picture he had of God was a commonplace one. An old
man, of that much he was sure. He was unable to say what colour
eyes or what sort of nose and mouth He had, but the long, white,
silken beard was clear in his mind. He sat on a throne like that of
George V, protected by angels' wings. At His feet, raising His
arms in an imploring gesture, was Jesus Christ. Meurig imagined
Him, day and night, interceding with His Father. He was almost

sure that His Father would forgive the sins of the world, but not quite. He had some cause for doubt and would spend eternity in intercedence lest something happen.

Meurig was aware that his fleeting mind needed strict discipline if he was to worship God truly, and so he drew up a number of rules which would have to be strictly kept. He decided to buy a copybook and write out two verses before leaving the house in the morning, to read at least one chapter of the Bible every night, to put his head down and shut his eyes tight during prayers, refuse the sweets his sister offered him in chapel, sing all the words of every hymn, give out the heads of the sermon and recite them in the deacons' seat, sit every Written Examination, and steer clear of boys of the same age. None of this was easy for his lively temperament and sometimes he kicked over the traces. He failed to resist Guto the Hendre's challenge to knock on the door of Marged Jones y Giât and then run away. His sister's caramels made his mouth water, and he succumbed. And one Sunday evening he closed his eyes too tightly during the prayer just before the sermon and his aunt had to dig him in the ribs. 'Aren't you ashamed of yourself?' she hissed between her teeth. He was perspiring profusely but, in fact, he almost laughed when he saw Guto doubled up with laughter.

But he did not allow his shortcomings to go unpunished. He had read in the Book of Martyrs[2] about men walking barefoot through the living flame, and of others who scourged themselves with thorns. There was a picture of one of them wallowing in horrible mire. The book said this would bring them peace. The burden of their sins would be lightened and they would know themselves purified and blessed in the grace of God after they had been scourged. He too would tame his God in the same way. Sometimes he wrote out four verses instead of two, or put his penny in the Missionaries' Box rather than spend it. Once his foot was caught so near the fire that a blister appeared on his leg. And that morning, after listening to Guto the Hendre telling of how he had helped his father with the lambing, he went to clean out the privy at the top of the garden. It put him off his dinner but he felt like Job[3] when he was raised from his dunghill into the antechambers of the Lord.

At fourteen Meurig was received into full membership of the chapel and took his first communion.

Up to this time his mother's death had been the most significant incident in his life. In one sense, looking back many years later, and considering the many events which had shaped him, he was certain that this had indeed been the most important. Others had had a deeper effect on him, but only for a while; he felt there was in her death something stronger than cause and effect, something other than a concatenation of ideas, binding them all together. This was the cornerstone of the whole, for this was the source of the great fear that had for years tormented and preyed on him, keeping him from sleep and turning every dream into a horrible nightmare.

Everyone in Llanifor had been surprised when his parents married, his mother more than anyone. She was the eldest of three sisters. The second sister had been joined in holy matrimony and in the fullness of time came home with a baby in her arms. 'She's her Mam's sugar-candy, every bit. Give your Auntie Gwen a kiss.' The youngest also came home with a baby soon after marrying. 'Who's a good boy, then? Of course you are. Give your Auntie Gwen a kiss.'

'Gwen, would you mind knitting some trousers and a coat for little Ifor? Ifor would like Auntie Gwen to knit trousers and coat for him, wouldn't you, my diddums?'

'Gwen, the trousers and coat you knitted for Ifor are lovely. Is there enough wool left to make a frock for Enid, I wonder?'

She was content to dandle her sisters' children in the belief that it was her fate so to do. It was useless to try flouting Providence. The proper and religious thing to do was to submit. Her days dragged by monotonously and she lost the strength even to wish for things to be changed. She got up with the maid and took tea and thin toast to her mother in bed. She sat at the head of table and poured her father's tea. She listened to him getting heated about the enthusiam of Tom Ellis and Lloyd George and Ellis Jones-Griffiths[4] for the rights of Wales, talking about disestablishing the Church, and glorifying God because He had revealed himself in an iceberg that sank the Titanic[5] as punishment for all the godless claims that had been made for it. She accepted it all quietly, without argument. During the daytime she would dust the dresser and mantelpiece to help the maid, and whenever she heard her father pounding on the shop wall, she would hasten into the passage in the knowledge that some woman wanted to buy a petticoat or stays.

She attended chapel regularly, but without ever being asked to do anything important: there were, of course, plenty of trivial things for her to do.

'Miss Davies, they've chosen you to go around the Corsydd and collect for the Foreign Mission. It's a boggy old place, I know, but it's so important that someone should go, isn't it? I'm sure you'll help us out. It will be a nice little walk for you.' She would return with her feet sodden and barely two shillings in her pocket for spreading the Gospel.

'Miss Davies, will you see that the plates are washed and the kettles clean for the Monthly Meeting, please? We know we can always depend on you.'

Often she would slip out of the village and make for Pant Rhedyn where the blackbird and dunnock are tamer. Or up to the Gwyllt with its strong beech-trees that are as pretty in winter as they are in spring, their bark the colour of lavender and shiny as brocaded silk. Of a still summer's day she would sit alone for hours. Birds alighted on her shoulder as upon a branch. Once a spider spun its web between her body and the trunk of a tree. And once she saw a dunnock fly to its nest and drop its own chicks' worm down the greedy throat of a young cuckoo.

When Thomas Lewis came to help her father in the shop during the Great War, Gwen was thirty-two, lifeless, drained of all energy, listless, heedless, with no shine in her eyes or colour to her cheeks. She went on with her monotonous tasks. She was content that her parents and sisters and even the maid took her for granted. She accepted the contempt of her acquaintances. And all this without sulking or bitterness, for deep, deep down – much too deep for her to be aware of it – something was stirring that would make life worth living. She had never realized that knowing the difference between a weasel and a stoat would make it possible for her to dust every day without going out of her mind. She would not have believed it if she had been told that seeing a dove's chick sticking its head down its mother's throat in search of food had made her raise her voice less often in the shop. Nor did she tell the minister's wife to run her own errands because a small skylark had come down yards from its nest, running towards it on its own path in order to mislead the observer.

Thomas Lewis had been turned down by the Army Medical Board and soon after coming to Llanifor the responsibility for the shop had fallen on his shoulders, for shortly afterwards John Davies had retired to a corner to read his newspaper, appalled that his heroes had lost their vision.

Thomas was a shopkeeper without peer. He organized the place into tidy departments – men's clothes here, women's there, children's and other small garments over there. The place was like a neat sermon with three heads to it. When he was put in charge of the shop he realized how important debt could be. He knew to the halfpenny how much credit to give this one and that in order to get them under his thumb. To put it in terms of Seilo's accounts, he considered the debts of those like the family at The Laurels, and the minister's wife's, to be assets. Many a time he derived a wanton satisfaction from seeing the latter in her expensive clothes and thinking it was only her naked body that her husband owned. There was even doubt on that score, so they said. He was as adroit at selling a handkerchief as a suit, and for him stays were as sexless as buttons. That was what had caught Gwen's attention in the first place.

'You don't have to come into the shop at all, Miss Davies, if you don't want to.'

'But what about...?'

'I've grown used to selling them over the years.' He smiled modestly. 'Of course, if we're busy, I should be very glad to have your help, but I'm sure you have more than enough work at home with your father and mother.' He spoke gently, sympathetically, in the voice he kept for funerals and other emotional occasions to do with the Ministry such as denouncing a drunkard or expelling someone from the Fellowship meeting.[6] Gwen was touched. 'Thank you, Lewis, thank you very much.' She noticed that his suit fitted him perfectly, that his shoes gleamed and that he had nice blue eyes and good teeth.

There was quite a bit of to-ing and fro-ing between the house and shop, and the narrowness of the passage often made for contact between them. Quite innocent at first – 'I'm sorry.' 'That's quite all right'; but as he came to realize Gwen's possible worth, it became not quite so innocent. He came into physical contact with her and every touch was like a piercing flame to her maidenhood. One day he kissed her, and from that moment he had no doubt. Thomas was an experienced lover – very experienced. He knew how to take less than he might have taken and within six months he had proposed and been accepted, much to the astonishment of the village, sighs of relief from Gwen's married sisters, and real gratitude on the part of her parents.

Soon after their daughter's wedding, as if the old were giving way to the young, John Davies and his wife both died. On his deathbed Gwen's father called for her.

'Gwen.'

'Yes, Father?'

'Come here.' He drew her to him and whispered in her ear as if sharing a secret. 'When he was given a job in the Cabinet, he forgot all about Wales.'

'He went very quietly,' she informed the minister's wife, 'though he was quite confused at the last.'

She was not disappointed in her husband. Starved of the pleasures of the flesh for so long, they became everything to her. If she had once disapproved of her younger sister, she now found it easy to forgive her. How lovely the urgency in the anticipation of passion, how exquisite the subsequent langour. She was like a healthy animal. Life returned to her dark eyes, colour to her cheeks and lips. Her black hair shone, she moved with nimble grace. She laughed often, a laugh that made the maid laugh, too, without knowing why, and encouraged her to ask for, and get, a whole week off instead of four days.

While she was carrying Meurig, her happiness was at full tide. It was as if years of indifference had stored up the unused energy and strength which were now enabling her to produce a strong, healthy child. She lost herself in her body, loving it passionately. It was like an old, valuable piece of china. Like her mother's three-part cupboard with the pewter plates. She looked in the mirror and noted with satisfaction that her face was slowly losing its shape and turning pale and long like that of a saint or monk, and that her breasts were growing heavy, and her loins.

She became shamelessly proud, haughty and arrogant. But sometimes she felt humble, and set apart. Like Mary. She read over and over the story of the angel of the Lord announcing the birth of John the Baptist and Jesus.[7] She forgot to put out crumbs for the robin in the garden. The tortoise died for lack of care and she was not sure whether she had heard the cuckoo that spring.

For nine months she even ignored the Great War. The slaughter and destruction, the cruelty and hatred, the arrogance and despair were as nothing compared with the baby inside her. The bravery and sacrifice did not touch her, and she was indifferent to the greed and rapine. She knew that the prosperous farmers of the district were growing as fat as their pigs and adding to their barns without thought of their immortal souls, but for all that she paid five shillings for a pound of butter without complaint. It was marrow for her bones, strength. She knew, too, that she and her husband were putting on weight at the expense of others, but lost not a wink of sleep because her whole mind was on her child. She sympathized with Lisa Parry of Gwern Afalau when the news came that Willy had been killed, but in her head she was singing, 'His name will be Meurig'. She was happy amidst the sadness, joyful amid the grief: in the midst of death, she was bringing forth new life.

The great happiness did not survive Meurig's birth, and Gwen never recaptured the passive, indifferent existence of the time before she was married – the existence which, for all its pointlessness, had given her a sort of enjoyment of which it could be said, at least, that it caused neither discomfort nor pain. She became more like someone else. She began to feel things more. She was more sensitive, more perceptive in her knowledge of people, more critical of them. The shamelessness of the minister's wife quite broke her heart as she sat drowsing for days trying to lessen the hurt. She picked on the small foibles of the maid and chastised her keenly. She discovered the natural kindness of Mrs Jones, her next-door neighbour – Shôs, as Meurig called her – who sang while she went about the housework, tickled Meurig on the soles of his feet, pressed his lower eyelid down to see whether there was anything in his eye, played at knock-the-door-look-through-the-window-lift-the-latch-and-come-inside, and put her finger in his gaping mouth.

Gwen came to know her husband and grew to detest him. She hated his servility in the shop; hated his false deference to The Laurels family; hated his blue eyes and good teeth; hated his sickening sanctimoniousness in the deacons' seat. Above all, hated herself for her frequent obeisance to him and the unruly lust which fuelled her hatred.

There were two poles to her life. Whenever she was offended or loathed herself more than usual, she pulled in her horns and sat for hours by the fire without the energy to wash or do her hair, peevish and quiet. But when Shôs made pickle or a piece of pancake, and brought some around for her, she revived and sprang to life again. She put on her clothes and went out for a walk, sometimes stopping and watching and listening, the wind in her hair and Meurig at her side struggling for breath.

'How's the woman at the shop these days?'

'Sulking all day long,' replied Meri. 'Isn't it a pity?'

'She was like a goat about the place last week.'

And poor Meurig forever caught between the two extremes.

When his mother sat dejected by the fire, he would push his little head between her arm and lap. There was coldness and hardness there, and the hammer of John the Dolydd blacksmith striking, striking, striking. And no sparks, as if the smithy were empty and the fire gone out, and he was too puny to work the bellows. Sometimes it was a robin redbreast in the depths of winter looking for crumbs in the snow, pecking here and there and finding nothing. It would leap onto the windowsill and peck against the pane, and no one noticed. He would remember the warm armpit of Shôs then, and run out through the back door.

'Shôs.'

'Yes, my love?'

'Shôs...' And into her arms, to be carried to the armchair.

'What have they done to you, my little one? Did they then, drat them all!' She would hug him tenderly and gently rock him, and the two black cats on either side of the mantelpiece would half shut their drowsy eyes, and Tom Tom in the middle would spur his white horse. 'Gee up, little horse, and carry us two over the mountain to gather nuts... gather nuts... gather nuts...'[8]

On another occasion she dragged him through the thickets of the Gwyllt, with nettles stinging his bare legs, the thistles pricking him, and goose-grass sticking to him, a fierce sun burning his face, and insects in his hair, up his nostrils and in his mouth, and a big bumble-bee buzzing around him, and the salt of his sweat in his eyes, and lead weights where his feet had been. He was unable to think. He was a body; flesh and blood; nothing else.

'Mam...'

'My little darling, did the nettles sting you then? Never mind... look...'

She picked some dock leaves and rubbed them until a green juice covered the white spots, and hugged him to her and kissed him over and over again; on his cheek, his forehead, his eyes, the nape of his neck, his lips. 'Mam, I'm afraid... what shall I do... no breath... I'm suffocating... Mam... don't... don't suffocate me...'

'Look, Meurig, a heron.' She let go of him, but he was too tired, too frightened, too exhausted, to see or hear anything. Then she dragged him back through the Gwyllt, through the nettles, through the thistles, through the brambles, through the ferns and rushes, his body hurting all over and his eyes shut tight.

'Shôs.'

'Yes, my love?'

'Shôs,' and he leapt into her arms.

But every now and again there were blessèd intervals of natural good temper, his mother smiling like Shôs, and speaking like her, and walking like her. He would lie in bed with his feet warm and the sheets turned neatly over the blanket lest it tickle his chin, while his mother folded his clothes which had been left in a heap at the foot of the bed and on the floor.

'Did you say your prayers, Meurig?'

'Yes, Mam.'

'And "put my head down to sleep?"'

'Yes, Mam.'

'Very well then, good-night.'

'Good-night.'

They were sitting by the fire, his father having gone to chapel and Meri the maid gone to see her mother. The fire burned brightly. The coal took the form of neither dragon nor wizard nor witch to frighten him — it was only coal. It gave out heat and nothing else. The wind slammed the door, rattled the window, made a racket in the chimney. The shadow in the corner was that of the dresser, and the noise was that of mice in the wainscote. His mother told him a story about Pwyll or Branwen or one about Arthur and the Round Table,[9] her voice like a teacher's, causing only pleasant, intelligible, mild excitement. The room was overflowing with good humour. Shôs was everywhere – on the hearth, in the fire, under the table, in his mother's bearing, in her eyes, in her voice.

'... and so she taught a starling to speak, and told him about Bran, her brother, and wrote a letter expressing her pain and disgrace... and hid it under the little bird's wing...'

She felt safe with her son in their sanctuary. Only Meurig and herself and the fire banked with coal, the curtains drawn and no one to see them; no one to see the happiness which had been building up in the parlour, the innocent happiness of a sheep and its lamb, the happiness of Aber Henfelen,[10] lost in time, the grief of having lost Brân receding, and the birds of Rhiannon singing.[11] Meurig's eyes were for her alone, eager to hear more. She knew that she could take her eyes off him and look up at the picture of her parents on the wall, or poke the fire, or stroke the cat, and when she looked back, he would still be watching her, his eyes trusting and adoring. She found great solace in this bond. She came into some money. She squandered it. She went on a spree of certainty, was intoxicated by the closeness between them, gave herself up to trust. Poverty would follow this. It would surely come, and famine, too, and a pale face, and greed and pain. What matter? She felt reckless, bold, daring. She would challenge Shôs.

'Do you want to go to Shôs?'

'To Shôs?' That was a strange question.

'I thought perhaps...'

'I'm glad Brân was in Caernarfon when the starling found him. What happened then, Mam?'

They were one like the Trinity. His breath was her breath. A good deal of the strength and irresponsibility and arrogance of the nine months she had carried him came back to her. It was as if he were in her womb for a second time.

The morning his mother died, Meurig went out of sight of the village and walked towards the Gwyllt. It was April and the vigour of spring had brought out the blossom and lambs; wild strawberries, primroses and buttercups grew in clusters under the hedges. He had not wept. He felt he should, but the tears would not come. He had seen his father wiping his eyes, unable to speak. Shôs was not crying either, and Meurig knew that his mother was more of a friend to her than to his father. He picked a buttercup and put it under his chin to see whether the pollen would stick there. He noticed how shiny the petals were, like mucus, and suddenly they turned on him as if they were some horrible food. He crushed a primrose and observed the many black insects that swarmed tirelessly at the base of the petals. He was astonished at how many times he had smelt the scent of primroses. He imagined the black creatures making their way up his nose and down his throat and through his whole body. He threw away the flower and stamped it into the earth. A few steps further on he saw a wren's nest, the first of the year. His heart beat with joy and he immediately stuck his finger into it. He was nervous. There is danger in a wren's nest. There is no way of knowing how deep it is, and the finger has to be crooked to feel the eggs there. There is no knowing what lurks in the darkness. A snake perhaps, the early warmth having woken it from hibernation. Suddenly he was weeping copiously. 'Mam wouldn't be afraid to put her finger into a wren's nest,' he said to himself.

He was still crying as he passed Fron Wen without noticing Elin Gruffydd leaning on the little gate.

'What's the matter, my boy? Are you feeling ill?'

'I've got a... a... sore throat...' He felt ashamed.

'You don't say. Wait a bit, I've got some sugar candy in the house. Nothing like it for a sore throat.'

Meurig accepted the sugar candy and ran home as fast as his legs would carry him.

Shôs took him up to the bedroom to see his mother in her coffin. He looked at her hands, the palm of one folded over the back of the other. They were dry, like firewood. He saw her teeth between her blue-black lips, the bruises under her eyes; on her forehead, attracted there by the stifling atmosphere of the room, a fly had settled. He thought of the buttercups and the primroses and the wren's nest, felt giddy and came close to fainting.

'Come along, my boy.'

But now he was well again, strong and unafraid. He tried to catch the fly between his finger and thumb, but it eluded him and flew away. Although he knew that corpses were cold, he was struck with terror when he touched his mother's forehead. It was cold like the eggs of a bird that has abandoned its nest. He thought, 'It will never come back to its nest.'

How many parts are there to a man? Two parts. What parts are they? Body and soul.[12] He saw her soul like the dove of the Holy Spirit on the cover of *Y Drysorfa Fawr*[13] flying away into the sky, far away from the body, flying and leaving its nest in anger.

'She'll never come back, will she, Shôs?'

'No, my darling, never.' For Shôs, Gwen and her soul were indistinguishable.

He was unable to drag himself away from the coffin. Dozens of memories flitted through his mind. Summer. He and his mother are sitting on the bank of Llyn-y-felin – a long strip of water with a stand of beeches on one side of it. It looks as if it is going to rain and swallows are flying low and skimming across the surface of the lake.

'They drink on the wing.'

'What?'

'The swallows, they drink in flight. They can wash themselves on the wing, too.'

It is a cold afternoon. He and his mother are on their way to the top of Clogwyn Glas. The biting wind is reddening her forehead and blowing her hair across her face. She stumbles on a stone and falls. She is unable to get up for a moment or two. Then she goes on her way and he follows her. At the top of the Clogwyn, far from everywhere, with the wind whirling around them and threatening to blow them away, she shouts out across the countryside. Just shouts and shouts.

'Mam, what's the matter?'

Her eyes are happy, she is smiling and there is colour in her cheeks. 'Nothing, my boy. I'd almost forgotten what my voice sounded like. Come on home.'

She draws her hand through his hair and runs down the slope.

The first part of a novel that was never finished; published in
Yr Arloeswr (rhif. 1, Haf, 1957)

Duty

The thorniest problem of my life has been to decide what exactly my duty is. I am sometimes jealous of the bold confidence of Mr Williams, our minister, who often of a Sunday morning shouts, 'Our duty as Christians... is such and such...!' The most innocent things cause me anxiety.

Take this morning, for instance, when someone called at the surgery to say a car had knocked down a small child next door to the post office in the High Street.

By the time I got there, there were a good dozen people fussing in front of the house – some in the front garden and others on the doorstep even. My first reaction was to send the nosey-parkers packing. But in their midst was Marged Jane from Foty Fach, down from the mountain on some errand, no doubt. She said not a word – just looked at me with her quiet, watery eyes like a cow's. How could I say anything unkind to her? Perhaps, deep inside her murky consciousness, she had some notion that she was being helpful. Duty number two – don't hurt the feelings of Marged Jane, or anyone else for that matter.

I said just now that I am jealous of the certainty of Mr Williams, the minister. Not always, by a long chalk. Uncertainty, perhaps, is a problem and a pain, but it gives life relish, too. That is why this evening I am on tenterhooks as never before.

This morning I received a letter from Philip Thomas, the manager of Linton's shop in Caerfabon. An amiable, harmless lad is Philip. But what's the matter with me? A lad, indeed! Philip is thirty-five if he's a day, and married for a second time. He has a little girl, Ruth, from his first marriage – how old is she, I wonder? Eight? – and a little boy of six months from his second, to Linda. Amiable, harmless, but often unable to control his feelings. You will see from the way he writes the excess of emotion – it's enough to make your hair stand on end. Listen to this:

Windy Ridge
Pine Grove
Caerfabon

Dear Dr Pugh,

I am the happiest man on earth this evening. After many a sleepless night and a sort of vague anxiety about Linda, the firmament of my life (one of Mr Williams's many platitudes) is once again cloudless.

Before me are cigarettes that have been only half-smoked – signs of Linda's anguish, but her hand, thank God, is on mine as I write, and her nails, I notice, are painted red — a sign of her new confidence. She is wearing the bracelet I gave her on our wedding day – her little way of showing we are making a fresh start. Why... Oh why... didn't she tell me the whole story from the start...?

But I am sure you won't be able to make head or tail of this story unless I explain how I was dragged into Philip and Linda's life. I shall come back to the letter.

How long is it? It's three years, or more, since I heard the night bell ringing. I went down and there at the front door was a woman. It was only afterwards I noticed how dirty she was. All I noticed at that moment was the horrible stench coming from her – something like a mixture of stale beer and slops.

'Please come at once, Doctor,' she said. 'At once, please... please...'

'Where to?' said I.

'To Red Walls.'

It may be difficult for you to believe this, perhaps, but although I knew of Red Walls, I had never been there – indeed, I thought no one lived there. Having seen the place, no one should live there either. A row of filthy stone houses.

I could hardly believe my eyes. A young girl with a mop of naturally blond hair and red-painted nails lay in the whitest bed I had ever seen, white, that is, except for the twin bloodstains big as the palm of your hand on the pillow. When she heard me the girl opened her eyes.

'There's nothing to fear,' I said.

'I'm not afraid,' she replied, somewhat petulantly. 'What's there to be afraid of, leaving a dump like this?'

She put her hand on the blood-stained pillow.

'The two reds don't match, do they?' she said, looking at her nails. 'You have to do something to keep up your self-respect.'

Somehow, in a flash, it dawned on me.

'Why do you stay here?' I asked.

'She's my mother.'

A plain answer, with neither bitterness nor love in it – only biological responsibility.

'An ambulance will be here in half an hour,' I said.

Rushing downstairs, I saw the mother suddenly shut a cupboard door and wipe her mouth with the back of her hand.

After a fortnight in hospital, Linda was almost fully recovered. She didn't say much but I was given to understand that she and her mother had only recently arrived in Caerfabon, and that they knew no one here and no one knew them. Strangely enough, as she got better she wasn't half so sure of herself – she was nervous, listless somehow.

For once, at any rate, I was sure where my duty lay. I couldn't let Linda go back to Red Walls, and after talking it over with my wife, I decided to give her the chance of making her home with us. She needed no persuading, and in a few days it was as if she'd always been with us. Fortunately, she was exceedingly quick with figures and just as clever as a secretary.

One day she caught me looking at her hands. Her nails had their natural colour. She gave me a slow smile.

'Varnish and self-respect don't go together any more,' she said.

One morning, a few days later, I was finishing my breakfast when my wife came downstairs.

'I'm afraid Linda's going to leave us,' she said. I couldn't believe it. 'She went out this morning without making her bed, taking last night's newspaper with an advertisement marked in it – Wanted. Cashier at Linton's, High Street, Caerfabon. Apply Philip Thomas, Manager.'

'But why?' I asked.

'Something I said last night, I'm afraid. When she came in from the pictures I happened to be in the hall. "Can you smell that strange smell, Linda?" I asked. "My past is a nightmare," she replied as she rushed past me up the stairs and slammed the door of her room.'

Well, there we are, we all say thoughtless things and regret it afterwards.

When she came back I didn't beat about the bush. I asked

her, 'Did you get the job?'

The old petulance came back into her eyes and just as abruptly she replied, 'Yes, I did.'

'Do you mind telling me how much you'll be paid?'

'Not at all. Four pounds ten shillings.'

'I'll give you ten shillings more,' I said.

She couldn't stop laughing. I put my hand on her shoulder.

'Linda, my dear, you'll have to learn to face up to your past. A crisis will come when you can't avoid it.'

'Let's wait until the crisis comes, shall we?' she said.

Weeks went by and Linda's nails stayed clean. While writing a letter for me one morning, she suddenly stopped and looked at me coquettishly.

'The visit to Linton's wasn't completely wasted,' she said.

'Oh?' I said, just as mischieviously.

'Philip Thomas has asked me to marry him.'

'And are you going to?'

'Of course.' And before I could say another word, she added, 'And, Dr Pugh, this isn't the crisis.'

'You know he has a little girl?'

'I've seen her often. A pretty little thing, half idolises her father but hates me.'

'It's a bit of a risk, Linda,' I said.

She ignored what I had said.

'The funny thing is, she's all over me with kisses when her father's about.'

'Little schizophrenic!' said I to myself.

And that's exactly what she was. From the first day after her father and Linda were married, Ruth lived two lives. She never lost an opportunity of irritating her step-mother – nothing too obvious, but anything to cause trouble; the minute her father came on the scene she was a little angel.

A few months before Linda's child was born, things came to a sort of head. She still went to see her mother and on this occasion, as soon as she returned, Ruth came in, and like all children who half-sing their sentences, said: 'Aunty Linda going to Red Walls... Aunty Linda going to Red Walls...'

Horrified, she gave the child a smack, undressed her and put her to bed. When her father came home, she was crying her eyes out.

'What's up?' he said.

'I smacked her,' replied Linda.

'Smacked her? What for?'

'Something she did.'

'Yes, but what?'

'What's it matter, as long as I thought she deserved it?'

Well, to cut a long story short, things went from bad to worse. Linda packed her bags and came here. I couldn't in all conscience refuse her a bed.

I shall never forget that night. Linda was stubbornly quiet now, half-smoking cigarette after cigarette, and my wife was worried as to whether she should write to Philip or not. What went straight to my heart was seeing Linda, determined and methodical, painting her nails red.

But I couldn't refuse the repentant Philip when he called here next morning and, like Menna Rhen,[1] back she went. As I saw her off in the car I asked, 'Was this the crisis, Linda?'

She frowned.

'One more try, Dr Pugh.'

And there was just one. Her little boy was born in May. His name is Ifor. That's my name, too. Ruth doted on him and was a lot less trouble to Linda — indeed, she helped look after her little brother. These were the least troubled weeks of Linda's marriage so far. Little did she think it was the calm before the storm.

Yesterday morning, she took Ruth out, with Ifor in the pram, to go shopping. She had a large parcel of dirty clothes to give to the woman who cleans the church and she left Ruth with Ifor. When she came back, there was no sign of either of them. She came straight here.

'I know where he is, Dr Pugh,' she said. 'Red Walls. Will you come with me?'

For once in my life I knew what my duty was.

'On one condition,' I replied. 'That we call at Linton's on the way.'

She looked at me for a moment.

'Is this the crisis, Dr Pugh?'

'Yes, Linda, this is the crisis.'

'But I can't say Ruth took him. Philip would break his heart.'

This time I wasn't so sure of my duty. To this day, I'm still not sure.

'What are you going to tell him?'

'I'll say Mam took him.'

Well, who am I to doubt the wisdom of certain fibs? And that's what happened: she called on Philip and told him what she wanted him to know. The child was amusing himself quite happily amid the odour of stale beer and slops, and Linda's mother too drunk to take any heed of him.

On the way home, Philip said to her, 'But why, Linda... why didn't you give me the whole story from the start? It wouldn't have made any difference to me. A storm in a teacup, as far as I can make out...'

He says the same thing in his letter, doesn't he? *Why... Oh why didn't she tell me the whole story from the start...?*

Tonight, as I read Ruth a story before she went to bed, and I saw her sweet eyes sparkling at me and her face a picture of young innocence, I couldn't hold back my tears or not thank God that my child has been spared the pain that Linda and I have suffered...

And now, what is my duty?

Storïau'r Deffro (gol. Islwyn Ffowc Elis, Plaid Cymru, 1959)

The Man from Groeslon

She wasn't, even at her best, quite all there, but sometimes, when I was a lad, the kink in her personality would break out in a bout of cruel fun at the expense of Groeslon people. Although, or perhaps because there were in the village, four chapels and a church, the outward signs at least of religion and morality, Catrin's occasional derangement took the form of highly vocal and active outbursts against the whole lot. Once, prowling at the back of the parsonage, she found a suspicious number of empty bottles – communion wine bottles, innocent enough, no doubt, though I would not swear to it. She carried them in her apron down to the main road and arranged them, as evidence, in a row along the wall, shouting at the top of her voice, 'Look, everyone, here are the secret vices of Roberts the Parson.'

Because I console myself that I am comparatively without mental flaw, I shan't, in these brief memoirs, go rummaging about like the deranged Catrin in a bid to reveal my many secret sins. I believe with Daniel Owen and Williams Pantycelyn[1] that the concealment of my shortcomings is necessary if I'm to live in reasonable harmony, not to say respectably, with my neighbours. I may not, it's true, have much hope of hiding them from heavenly justice, assuming such a thing exists, but as for the common people, for my part, they can wait for someone else to expose me. And that's a pity, for it's a man's sins that make him interesting. Without sin there would be no literature. Aristotle,[2] almost the first of our literary critics, realized this when he defined the tragic hero as a man of great and heroic possibilities but with a blemish in his constitution. It is the blemish that's important to a writer. The goodness of the evil man is a sentimental commonplace, but the blemish in the good man is a necessity of the human condition.

Nor do I intend being tidy and to proceed in chronological order. I shall mix the past, about which there's nothing to complain except that it's frighteningly fleeting, with the present, which is so brief that it hardly exists, and the future which is now inevitably short and its days numbered – I shall mix regret and hope in one untidy mess.

Now, where to begin? The best and only place to start is by
confessing that I ought not to be so bold as to dare trace my past
at all. There ought to be some justification for venturing on such
a task. A man should have a past worth writing about, or else he
should have a unique personality which amuses the reader on
account of its arbitrary distinction, or because his life has
somehow changed the state of things for better or for worse, or
because he has thrown light on the past in a historical or social
or literary way, by his actions or by contributing to or providing
inspiration or pleasure. But I cannot, like Ida Haendel,[3] the
violinist, see in my past a way of explaining what I am today. I
have not, like Anais Nin, written erotic books to pay for the
upkeep of my children. And although I'm a bachelor, I've never
done anything as philanthropic as Peter Jeffcock, also a bachelor,
who brought up twelve children for London County Council.
It's not, mind you, that I am not shameless enough to believe that
some of my former pupils are a bit richer in their understanding
because of me, nor that I don't harbour some hope that certain
of my short stories and plays will not expire with me. But in
essence and to all intents and purposes, I am, like T.S. Eliot's
Gerontion,[4] very ready to acknowledge:

> I was neither at the hot gates
> Nor fought in the warm rain,
> Nor knee deep in the salt marsh, heaving a cutlass,
> Bitten by flies, fought.

I have been, and still am, a timid, innocent little creature.
Nothing heroic, nothing really adventurous, has ever happened
to me. Whatever grief or joy, whatever excitement or bliss I've
experienced, has all taken place within the confines of my own
home and among my acquaintances, without affecting anyone or
anything else.

As a boy I was like a baby, afraid of my own shadow, wrapped
tightly in swaddling clothes by my parents, my grandmother and
my Uncle John. I never felt at ease and free and happy among
lads of my own age. They were bold and venturesome. I remember feeling very jealous when some of them were refused full
membership of the Fellowship[5] at Brynrodyn and were put 'on

probation', as it were, because they'd been up to some mischief at the station in Groeslon, tormenting the stationmaster. Their irresponsible defiance had the same effect on me as Wil Bryan had on Rhys Lewis.[6] I used to live their lives by proxy, carrying out the most dangerous feats in my imagination, challenging parents and society alike. That's why, perhaps, I find it difficult, painfully so indeed, to devise plots in my plays. Practical action is no part of my nature. It's so much easier for me to live in the minds of other people than to show them in action. My life has been happy but colourless – another obstacle to writing interesting autobiography. Apart from the inevitable loss that comes in Death's wake, nothing really cruel has ever happened to me.

Just over a year ago, I had a nasty accident in America, and found myself in hospital at Rochester, Minnesota. The driver of the car was killed. It is a heartless thing to have to admit, but I now look back on the incident not with grief alone. It brought me experiences I should never have otherwise had. As I was coming to in the accident ward, standing on one side of my bed was Dr Howell, a Welshman whose roots are in Llanbryn-mair, a cousin of Mrs O.V. Jones of Menai Bridge. On the other side, holding my hand and speaking to me in Welsh, was Dr Shorter from Ferndale, a niece of Mrs Morris who was for many years my neighbour in Groeslon – both of them doctors at the Mayo Clinic. Amazing, isn't it? And quite an unsettling little warning to my rational mind.

It's deeper than that, even: I have always been easy prey to the fear of dying, tossing and turning in my bed in a waking nightmare, dreading the inevitable helplessness that makes a mockery of life – a ridiculous waste of time, by the way, since I've almost used up my threescore years and ten! But lying there in my bed in Rochester with everything spinning like a wheel, unable to move, convinced I'd broken my back and that I'd never see Wales and Groeslon and Angorfa and my kinsfolk and friends again, and despite feeling downhearted and lachrymose, I knew no fear whatsoever. Perhaps my mind was not functioning properly. Anyway, I've now managed to persuade myself that when the time comes I shan't be afraid. It's fear that's the great bogey.

The accident also brought me comic experiences. As a bachelor, I've always been coy about my body, but, at the complete mercy – and it was blessed mercy, too – of the nurses at the hospital, I cared not a whit what anyone did to me. It's funny to think that pretty, feisty young Filipinos have seen parts of me that no other woman except my mother and grandmother have ever gazed upon — as far as I'm aware! I also came to realize how kind people are. So many visited me after I came home that Rachie, my cousin, who looked after me so well, remarked, 'John, now you've seen everyone who'll be at your funeral'.

Are early memories imagined or real, I wonder? The details are imagined, perhaps, but the overall impression is reliable enough. They are a kind of literature, drawing their background and actions from various places, various occasions and various times, but crystallizing some impression, some experience, indeed some incontrovertible fact. The farther away the memory, the more alive it is, a small creation independent of its time and place and now a permanent part of one's personality.

I was born: neither I nor anyone else can deny that. And although, like the existential atheists, I believe life to be a futile, aimless, meaningless condition, I am very, very glad that I *was* born. Life in itself is worth having, art for art's sake: at least, it's been worth having in my case. It's like some rare delicacy which does no good whatsoever to a man's body but is irrationally tasty. And bearing in mind that the bitter and the sweet are equally delicious.

My father was born at Bwlchderwin, but his family later moved to Penrallt at Clynnog. He was one of ten children and his mother one of fifteen. My father's family are legion and I am constantly being surprised to discover that so-and-so turns out to be a relative of mine. One of his cousins, Auntie Polly, married a son of Owen Thomas of Liverpool, so a cousin of Saunders Lewis[7] is a second cousin of mine! I remember my grandparents well: Taid was a mild, bearded creature while Nain – and it was the worst offence to say this in the presence of my father – was, to me, anyway, a quite vexatious and distinctly peevish woman. She could sit on the settle near the fire for days on end without a word to anyone. I once got a smack on the backside from her for stealing sweets which were kept in a bottle in the bottom drawer of a chest. Nain Penrallt and I did not have much to say to each other. And when I grew up a bit and had something to sulk about, my mother would be cross and say, 'Hey, out of my sight, you're starting to take after your father's family now!' It was no use being downhearted when Mam was around.

Mam was from Llandwrog and her mother was the daughter of Tai Gwynion, whose father at the time lived in the village. They were cousins. According to Taid, or so they say, it's foolish to keep someone else's family. Perhaps it is, but it can also have strange consequences. A few years ago I saw in one of the Sunday papers that a genetics researcher in Oxford was asking bachelors whose grandparents were cousins to get in touch with him. So I wrote to him and received a reply thanking me for providing yet more evidence for his theory that the genes of grandparents thus related turn up randomly in their grandsons – though not in their grand-daughters, mark you. It's a fine thing to be able to blame someone else for my being a bachelor – if anyone has to be blamed, since being a bachelor is no bad thing in itself! At least I shan't cause any real grief or be missed when I'm dead and gone.

My grandfather was always a sort of mythical hero for me. He died at the age of forty and my acquaintance with him therefore depends on my mother's memories. She was twelve at the time of his death, after which she had to go into service in Liverpool. As a consequence, she spoke fluent English with exactly the same accent as Cilla Black's,[8] though grammatically much more precise. As for my father, he had no English whatsoever, or only enough to reel off 'I believe in God the Father', which he had learned by rote at Ysgol-yr-Arch and would sometimes recite to hilarious effect. But to return to Taid. He was evidently a man with protest in the marrow of his bones. A quarryman, he'd walk all the way from Llandwrog to his work at Llanberis; he was the only quarryman in the village – everyone else worked for Lord Newborough on the Glynllifon estate,[9] and when they died they were given a free coffin as a bonus for a lifetime's labour. In the days of the Church Tithe, the Groeslon quarrymen made an effigy of Mr Jones, the rector of Llandwrog, carried it in a coffin and burned it in front of Ty'n Llan, the public house. Glynllifon had caught wind of their plan and the warning went out to everyone to draw their curtains and, on pain of losing their jobs, not to go near the place. But my grandfather went, taking my mother, a small child, by the hand. Next morning he was given notice to quit his house. He came to live in Groeslon and it was there he died. My grandmother then moved to Caedoctor in Llandwrog, the place which holds golden memories for me.

I'm pleased this happened to my grandfather and, being a great believer in genetics, take it as an explanation of the relish for protest in my own nature – something, by the way, that increases and turns ever more fierce as I grow older. The philistine stubbornness, sickening servility and pathetic childishness of those who, like Malvolio,[10] have had 'greatness thrust upon them' here in Wales in recent times have infuriated me more than anything else. There was a time when I was an out-and-out pacifist, and I'm still against the use of violence, whether it endangers lives in public buildings in Wales or in the vicinity of reservoirs, or whether it stems from the policy of a Government, be it red or blue, that sells arms to Nigeria yet does not raise a finger against the atrocities in Vietnam lest it upset the United States, but I have been obliged to realize that some people do not have the ability or the courtesy to listen to reasonable appeals. Nothing works with such people except to frighten them into acting justly. There is such a thing as constitutional violence.

As I see it, that's what History is all about. According to Collingwood,[11] the task of the true historian is to discover a principle which repeats itself down the centuries. One undeniable principle is that protest is inevitable if change is to be brought about and injustice removed. It can be seen running like a silver thread which binds the ten plagues of Egypt to the painting out of English signposts in Wales. What else are Martin Luther, Bunyan, Wilberforce, Parnell, Mrs Pankhurst, the Daughters of Rebecca, Jac Glanygors and John Penry?[12] How else were the foundations of the Labour Party laid? By sufferance and tolerance? Not on your life! It's true that pain and suffering and distress and cruelty are also associated with the principle. It has its Robespierre and its Hitler and its Stalin, but as Berdyaev[13] said, as a Christian dealing with the revolution in Russia, 'I should not like to give the impression that the reawakening in Russia was all corruption. It had its healthy symptoms as well.'

To me, the tragedy of life – the foul paradox of man's condition – is that tolerance, the ability to live in other people's minds, credos and convictions which are diametrically opposed to your own so that you acknowledge that they have just as much a right to their views as you have, is a great ideal. The sad thing is, if this principle is accepted, you become a static, uncreative eunuch. The fanatical element, the conviction that you alone are right, is essential if progress is to be made in this old world. That was the course of W.B. Yeats's[14] development as a man and poet. He first escaped, as a gilded intellectual, into the slack aestheticism of Innisfree, but when the Irish dam broke in 1916 he had to acknowledge that a man is incomplete if he lacks ferocity, that this and the destructive element in his nature can be as creative as meekness and tenderness.

> You that Mitchel's prayer have heard,
> 'Send war in our time, O Lord!'
> Know that when all words are said
> And a man is fighting mad,
> Something drops from eyes long blind,
> He completes his partial mind.

The mind of the poet Robert Williams Parry[15] became whole in this way. The pretty sweetness of his early verse turned to fury and he lashed out mercilessly: 'Take up thy bed and walk, O Wind,' he wrote, and urged the angry wind to flay the lukewarm, the unrepentant and the apathetic. If he were alive today, he'd have no lack of targets.

My grandfather was also a cultured man, it seems. I have in my possession a number of clever essays which he wrote on Biblical subjects in lively language and a copperplate hand. He was, too, an accomplished musician. His stopless harmonium is still a cherished piece of furniture in my home. He learned sol-fa with Ieuan Gwyllt[16] and passed on its mysteries to my mother. I can't recall a time when I wasn't able to read sol-fa – soffeuo as Mam used to call it – and I found it a very handy and lucrative way of earning a penny at the Band of Hope by using it to go up and down, back and forth, on the modulator. When Taid passed away, a prize was given at the literary meeting in Bwlan for an elegy for him; it opens with this inspired couplet:

Mr John Williams yn anfarwol ac yn huno'i hun o hedd,

The Plum Tree

Er bod gwyntoedd llawer gaeaf wedi rhuo dros ei fedd!

(Mr John Williams is immortal and sleeps in heavenly peace / Though the winds of many winters have roared over his grave!)

As for my grandmother, my mother's mother, I don't know whether I'm idealizing her, but for me she was perfect. She was a tall, healthy, jolly countrywoman with a rough-hewn face the colour of ripe corn, unable to speak a word of English, who wore a flowery bonnet to chapel, where she went of a Sunday evening not because it was vital for her immortal soul but because she liked going and enjoyed strolling there and back with anyone who would accompany her and help her to set the world aright. Above all, she defined wrong-doing differently from Mam. If I had wet my feet in the Caedoctor river, well, she gave me dry stockings, not the rough edge of her tongue. Because I wasn't fond of bread-and-milk or beaten egg, well, all right, she would let me have something more to my liking – a treacle sandwich or a griddle cake – instead of going on and on about the health-giving properties of the cow or hen. There were, however, some things which were forbidden in her house. Onions, for instance. My grandmother, my mother and Uncle John detested onions. As for me, they made my mouth water, and still do. There's nothing quite like the smell of onions frying. On Saturday nights I would slip next door to the home of Mary Jones, who would have been to town (I mean Caernarfon), a leisurely if bumpy journey in the brake. There, sizzling in a pan, I'd find onions with black pudding and sausages and liver, or lights as Mary Jones called them, a greasy mess that made my heart rejoice. I would scoff it down with the help of a slice of bread and fresh butter before slinking back in my unrepentant guilt to my grandmother's house. 'Where've you been?' John would ask. I wasn't allowed to call him Uncle or address him with the formal you. 'Mary Jones's house.' 'What did you have?' – and he knew full well. 'Sausages, black pudding, lights and onions,' I would reply, as if reciting a piece of poetry. 'You dirty little scavenger,' he would say. 'Dirty little scavenger,' and Nain would laugh.

My grandmother had for years looked after an old uncle of hers for years who'd been born a cripple and never walked –

cerebral palsy, probably. The first time my mother went to Caedoctor after I was born, old Uncle Harri took me in his arms and said, 'I'm only ninety years older than Jane's boy.' A few weeks later he was dead and, naturally enough, he left everything he had to Nain. This caused her brother, William, to take offence and for as long as they lived Nain never spoke to him again, although my mother and John were quite friendly towards him. Then it was Nain's turn to die. She had said, scores of times, 'I'm so hale and hearty, I really don't know what will come to carry me off.' But come it did. Cancer. She was lying in her bed in the front room with her face a sickly instead of a healthy yellow. There was a knock at the door and my mother went to open it. Who was there but Uncle William. 'I hear,' he said, 'that Elin's very ill.' 'Yes, she is,' said my mother, shaking like a leaf. 'I'd like to see her,' he said. 'Oh,' said my mother, afraid to ask him into the house. But Nain could see from her bed into the kitchen. My mother went into the bedroom. 'Uncle William's here,' she said. 'Wants to see you.' Nain replied, 'Tell him I've lived these thirteen years without speaking to him and I can die without speaking to him, too.' Despite this – no, to tell the truth, because of this – Nain remains perfect as far as I'm concerned.

The quarter mile around Caedoctor was heaven for me. Only there was I fearless and free, on my own, a veritable giant without having to compete with anyone. There were plenty of gnarled, branchy trees to climb, and if, after a struggle, I failed to climb them, no matter, there was no one to call me cissy, nor anyone to tell me off for tearing my clothes, either. There was a river with deep, dangerous pools in it, where I lay down on the stones in midstream to tickle and catch trout. There was a bottomless pool in the field at Cefnrhengwrt on which to skate in winter. It used to freeze much harder in days gone by, believe me! I used to swing fearlessly from the brittle branches of a plum-tree and pick the fruit for Nain to make jam. Sometimes I would venture further afield, to where the river ran into the sea past Glanrafon in the direction of the Belan fort, with the handles of a shovel and fork tied together to catch plaice. In the water, my feet tightly pressed together but leaving room between the soles, I waited for a small plaice more innocent than the others to slip in to be stabbed. I risked the marshy land of Nant

Cae Ffridd in a bid to pick a daffodil or iris more provocatively inaccessible than the rest. I thought I was the broth of a boy because I stole beans or peas or swedes or turnips from the field of Cefnrhengwrt, though I knew full well in my bones that, even if I were to be caught, Wil and Mag Jones would only say, 'Well, my lad, why didn't you say you wanted some?'

There was no one to laugh at me if I felt like catching wasps in a jampot or gathering primroses or buttercups or quaking grass or wild strawberries or blackberries. Blackberrying is still, for me, an enchanting pleasure. No one laughed at you, by the way, for gathering nuts. Odd, isn't it? I slept in the loft, and early in the morning, half-awake, heard next door's cows restless in their chains and the mare with its monotonous rhythm turning and turning the wheel of the churn; and when a shaft of light came through the skylight, I read *Cymru'r Plant* and *Cymru Coch*[17], copies of which I kept in the chest under the bed. There was one book in particular – the story of the Red Bandits of Mawddwy.[18] I have since searched for it all over, to no avail. It's just as well, I suppose, lest re-reading it might bring disillusion. Mercifully, neither Nain nor Mary Jones nor the trout nor the plaice nor the peas nor the beans nor anything belonging to Caedoctor comes back to disenchant me. They are preserved for ever, without flaw, in the glass case of my memory.

Not a week passed without my going from Groeslon to Llandwrog. I used to walk along the Lôn Glyn, as it was known, with the Glynllifon Wall on one side of me for exactly a mile, the wall being a circle seven miles in circumference to prevent the hoi polloi from tainting the hallowed halls of the Honourable F.G. Wynne.[19] I remember once plucking up enough courage to sneak through the gate of the Upper Lodge into the park. If you were caught there, it was the Clio for you (the Clio was the borstal of those days). I have had only one nightmare in my life and that was being caught by the gamekeeper in the park. On this occasion I saw nothing that was really frightening, but somehow or other I'd become friendly with Stanley Farmer, who lived at the Lodge. In his company I saw all the Honourable's eccentric playthings. There was a dogs' cemetery with a real church in it – blasphemy, my mother said. Don't talk nonsense, said Nain. There was a live eagle and a huge mansion and a fort full of old weapons. Through the Dingle flowed the river Llifon, swarming with fish and, on either bank, fern baskets that were famous all over the world, so they said. Best of all was the long cave, Cilmyn Droedd-ddu, and its meandering, damp dark until you came to the end where, in the roof, a pane of blue and red glass cast a mysterious light on the image of a little boy peeing. For an innocent child in those days to see a gadget for making water amounted to a forbidden perversiont that was magically and daringly pleasurable.

Once I went around the outside of the house itself and saw through a tall window the famous little train with which the Honourable used to play. All over the place there were small, colourful images such as the Seven Dwarfs, and gargoyles, and once I saw the Honourable high priest himself in a long black cape. He was just like one of the gargoyles, the ugliest creature I ever saw, despite his being a direct descendant of the Bourbons, if Maria Stella, his great-grandmother, was to be believed. Today the Caernarfonshire County Council owns Glynllifon, and it houses Theatr Fach Eryri, the drama company in which I take a great interest. Believe me, being able to visit it and walk around as if I own the place, up the wide staircase from the entrance hall, is a sort of miracle as far as I am concerned. I take sadistic pleasure in imagining the Honourable spinning in his grave.

I was born in Groeslon, high enough up the hill to see Caernarfon castle and the Belan fort and the beach at Newborough in Anglesey, its sand glistening as if it were always summer there. Looking up country, you can see Cilgwyn and the Foel and Mynydd Grug. I have never had much idea about north and south, east and west. For me, everywhere is either up or down, to the left or to the right. Life in Groeslon, compared with that in Llandwrog, was like wearing your Sunday suit all the time. You had to watch out. You had to have discipline. The words Don't and You Must were everyday words for me. You had to be a good boy. I shouldn't like to give the wrong impression, for all that. No boy was happier than I in my home life. When, as often happened, I was disobedient – another familiar word – I'd get a quick box about the ears from my mother and that was that. It was she who had to take charge of things because my father was a stonemason and had to follow his trade wherever it took him, sometimes as far afield as Holyhead.

Next door lived Shôs. I could never call her Mrs Jones, though that was her real name. In her house was a rocking-chair and in the little bedroom at the top of the stairs John M, her husband, kept a live bird with a real nest in which it laid eggs. Shôs was Llinor's mother and it was she who took me to school for the first time and kept an eye on me. It was Llinor who would spit on my hair and make a quiff in it whenever the photographer came round. Years later I was best man at her wedding. Shôs died young, when she was about thirty. Hers was the first death I remember properly. I was crying my eyes out on my way home from school. 'What's the matter?' asked Mrs Roberts, who lived at Tal Llyn Bach, though she knew full well. 'I've got a sore throat,' I said. 'Well, never mind, love. Just a minute, I've got some sugar-candy in the house. That will cure it.' The only sugar-candy to get rid of that kind of sore throat is Time. Next door on the other side lived Mrs Williams, mother of David Edmund and Hannah Mary and Morris Thomas, later the husband of Kate Roberts.[20] Mrs Williams had been in service with some toffs in Liverpool, in Everton Village, if I remember rightly, and she knew how to make things with strange names like ketchup and chutney. On Shrove Tuesday she'd make pancakes in a large earthenware bowl with a yellow band round its rim.

Hannah Mary and I still eat ketchup and chutney and pancakes in bitter-sweet remembrance of times past. In Mrs Williams's house there was a copy, big as the Bible, of *The Pilgrim's Progress*.[21] Whenever I was playing up because my mother wouldn't take me to the Llanllyfni fair I would be sent to her house to look at a picture that scared the living daylights out of me – a full-page picture of sinners wallowing in the mire of John Bunyan's Vanity Fair. 'Do you want to go to a place like that?' The truth was yes, I did. Strange how things change. A few years later only an earthquake would have kept my mother from Llanllyfni fair. All through my childhood she had convulsions, sometimes quietly for an hour on end before letting out a long sigh and coming to. All I could do was rush next door and, in a voice which Mrs Williams recognized as warning of my mother's fit, shout, 'Mrs Williams!' She would be there like a shot, whatever she happened to have on the go. My memory of neighbours in Rathbone Terrace (Rathbone, by the way, after William Rathbone,[22] the Member of Parliament), is one of kindness, geniality and unfailing neighbourliness. Not that there weren't some who were quite comic. My mother dare not hang my nappies on the line overnight, or she'd see them a day or two later on someone else's clothesline!

Looking back now, it seems to me that the great difference between today and when I was a child is that it never occurred to me to doubt the things which Convention had decreed as the imperatives of life. It was a time of unquestioning acceptance with no sense that a man's freedom was being impinged upon or his personality impaired. It was not that men did not revolt, but that they did so only as individuals. In essence they accepted the *status quo* as being eternally right. If I disagreed, that was my whim, a sort of personal irresponsibility on a small scale. Going to chapel three times on Sunday and at least twice on week-days to the Fellowship and the Prayer Meeting, and in winter to the Band of Hope and the reading classes to prepare for the examinations of the Children's Singing Festival and the County Examination, was as fundamental as eating or sleeping. Not, mind you, that I liked going – to be honest, I detested it, but I also detested rice-pudding and jacket potatoes and asafoetida and rhubarb and spirits of nitre (amonium nitrate). But it was my contrary individual nature that was responsible for my dislike, not the things themselves.

Of all the chapel meetings, the Fellowship was my asafoetida. We had to learn passages from the Bible while the Sunday sermon was going on and then the various heads for recitation at the start. Afterwards we had to sit, silent and uncomprehending, for three-quarters of an hour or more while the minister came down to enquire about the experiences of members. 'Has something been on your mind, Mary Jones?' he would ask. 'I've been thinking how good God is to me. God is my refuge and my strength, of ready assistance in every tribulation.' 'Yes, indeed; very good, very good.' And I knew all along that Mary Jones was living on the parish.

I'm still terrified whenever I recall the minister, the Reverend Arfon Jones, having the awesome idea that it would be useful if the young people were encouraged to pray, for which purpose he arranged a Prayer Meeting. I was old enough by this time to indulge my own whims and I would go only if dragged. Only once was I asked to take part, and the experience is branded on my mind. There I was on my knees with my nose pressed against the back of the pew in front, searching desperately for words. Although I'd listened to hundreds of public prayers – my father, by the way, would always end his with 'Forgive us our short-comings of every kind' – I could think of nothing to say. The cruel silence was broken by stifled squeaks of laughter. So I decided to say the Lord's Prayer, only to break down after a phrase or two, so that I got to my feet in a bath of sweat and shame and wretchedness. At the same time, I made an irrevocable decision: that was the first and last time I would pray in public. So it proved. The occasion will perhaps provide the psychologist with an explanation of my present condition.

I recall a similar occasion when I was accepted as a full member of the chapel, with the right to partake of the bread and wine to the accompaniment of the harmonium playing, out of tune and in a minor key, '*Cof am y cyfiawn Iesu*'. I was one of about a dozen who'd learned the appropriate parts of the Bible and some gobbledegook from the Confession of Faith and in the Fellowship had answered the Catechism before the fateful Sunday evening. I was sitting in the pew nearest the deacons' seat and trembling like a leaf. What on earth was I going to say as I bowed my head? No idea. But suddenly I got one that was, if nothing else, original: I would watch Robert Owen (Shân Emlyn's[23] father, by the way), the most cultured deacon of them all, and count for how long he kept his head down. One, two, three, four, slowly all the way up to twenty-three after the bread and to twenty-six after the wine. So twenty-three after the bread and twenty-six after the wine was my contribution that Sunday evening, too, whatever or whoever it was that demanded my veneration and respect. Blasphemous? Unseemly? Disrespectful? Ignorant? Unforgivable? All of these, perhaps, according to your convictions, but at the time, it was true. It wasn't something to swank about or take pride in; indeed, I can't deny it was really disgraceful that I'd deprived myself of the only experience in life that's worth having. But I must acknowledge that, ever since I began thinking not only rationally but also emotionally, I have never felt there's anything with which I can enter into personal communion except my fellow-man and his literary works.

Mercifully, the Chapel had its pleasures. One was the annual Literary Meeting. As it happened, I was fairly certain of winning the singing competition for my age-group. My mother used to coach me. I had a feeble little voice like a nestling's but it was clear and true when I sang '*Plant bach Iesu Grist a Duw*' and '*Clywch gân y dryw bach / Mor uchel ac iach*' and '*Ym mhreseb Bethlem Jiwda / Duw cariad Yw / Ym marw ar Galfaria / Duw cariad yw*'. After that I'd wait expectantly and confidently for the adjudication. 'The boy who sang second: a small voice, perhaps, but a most melodious one; splendid articulation and the top notes reached with ease. He is clearly the winner.' Then, pretending to be shy, I'd go up onto the stage for my threepenny bit and white rosette, thrilled to bits and wallowing, behind my mask of humility, in the applause. Years later, in 1939, at the Eisteddfod in Denbigh, when I was lucky enough to win the Drama competition and, for a novel, the Prose Medal[24] for a novel, despite the reference to me in one of the newspapers as 'a shy middle-aged man', I was aware that I was still the same person – the same thrill, the same mask.

I never won at recitation. I was really hopeless at it. I was once placed second for reciting some verses about a little dog that barked. It seemed I could bark better than the others. Isn't it ironic, to say the least, that for years I've been shameless enough to adjudicate recitation competitions at Eisteddfodau – at the National, even! At the Literary Meeting, too, I was quite sure of winning every written competition for my age-group and would come home plastered with white rosettes and a few red and blue ones too. On my own dunghill I was cock of the roost.

But it was a different story when it came to the examinations of the Children's Festival. This was for the whole area and the competetion was much tougher. Among my rivals was Tomos – Dr Thomas Parry[25] now – a lifelong friend. We competed in the same age-group, since he's only six weeks older than me. He always came first and I would be struggling to be placed second, and that didn't always happen either. But whether I was placed second or third, I still have a soft spot for the annual Children's

Festival to which we paraded under our streaming banners. Looking back, I realize it was there I instinctively began weaving the experiences and sensuous and personal impressions of my own life into the making of a story. This is how it happened. I was a ludicrously timid child. If I woke up at night, the silence and pitch-darkness would make me tremble with uncontrollable fear. I'd get up and feel my way gingerly around the bedside, find the door and pad across the landing's cold linoleum to the front bedroom to snuggle up between my parents till morning. Next day I'd be scolded: 'You're sure to fall down the stairs and break your leg and catch a cold and pneumonia. Is that what you want?' That occurred scores of times. On one occasion the question at the Festival was 'Relate the story of Eli and Samuel'.[26] I still remember the adjudicator, Mr Parry, the Penygroes schoolmaster, reading out my answer and everyone laughing – it went something like this: 'When Samuel was asleep in the house of Eli he heard a voice calling him and he rose and went into Eli's room. "Here I am," he said. "What is it?" said Eli. "You called," replied Samuel. "No, I did not. Go back to your bed." And Samuel went. Then he heard a voice calling him again and went into Eli's room through the darkness along the landing. "No, I did not call," said Eli. When he lay down again, Samuel heard a voice calling him for the third time and ran barefoot across the landing. "What's the matter with you?" asked Eli, growing angry. "Now, no more of this nonsense. You're sure to fall down the stairs and break your leg and catch a cold and pneumonia. Is that what you want?"' I was placed second that time too.

The other thing that couldn't be avoided, of course, was school, education: the divine fare which was to keep my hands clean and soft instead of calloused like those of my stonemason father. It was my mother who thought like this, not my father. She it was who laid down the law and groomed and advised me. My father never laid a finger on me and only ever offered me one piece of advice. 'Remember,' he said, 'to go to the lavatory every day even if all you do is sit there for a while.' According to a doctor writing in *The Times* last Sunday, keeping waste in the large gut for too long is one of the causes of cancer. Fair play to my father, a keen reader of every Welsh newspaper, as well as commentaries and biographies.

The Man from Groeslon

The first school I attended was at Penfforddelen. This Elen was probably Elen Luyddawg,[27] though it was some years after leaving the school I realized as much. I wouldn't say the place was anti-Welsh. Miss Sarah Ann Grey, the infants' teacher, who was from Llanelli, taught us arithmetic through the medium of Welsh and in a most lively, ingenious way. 'This is House One,' she would say, 'and here's House Ten. We'll start at House One. Now, four and three (chorus of Seven!), seven and five (chorus of Twelve!). There we are, twelve. We'll put two down here under House One. But what shall we do with this little one that's left? Perhaps there's room for him in House Ten. Let's knock on the door and see. Is there room for a little Ten here? Yes, come in.' And in he went. Good, isn't it?

I remember a huge, colourful wooden horse being brought to the school. Miss Williams, pale-skinned and rosy-cheeked, pretty as a flower, marshalled the knights. She had a cute way of teaching Geography. The further away the place you could name, the longer the ride on the horse. 'California,' was what I always said. My mother had a cousin who had run off to America – a paternity case, no doubt. When word reached us years later, it came from California. The name, without my knowing where the place was, had a special charm for me. Eighteen months ago, after a two-day, two-night journey in a train from Chicago – Miss Williams was fair enough in giving me a long ride – through heavy snow with only the stumps of cactus and clusters of ramshackle hovels visible from the carriage window, I reached California. Like Cortes,[28] I was thrilled to see the Pacific for the first time, despite the fact that the shoreline was quite similar to that of the Llyn peninsula. I was also astonished by a fantastic land of freeways and surprised to find smog where I had expected golden summer all year round.

From the infants' school I went on to the primary school where William Ellis was in charge: a short man, rotund and red-headed, who owned a small dog called Gyp. The mere sight of Gyp was enough to send us Groeslon children packing. Whenever our paths crossed in the street, William Ellis would ask me, in Welsh, how my parents were, but I heard nothing save English from him at school. His wife was an Englishwoman. I remember her and the parson's wife standing at our door and asking my mother to sign a petition against the Disestablishment of the Church in Wales.[29] 'Not on your life,' said Mam. From the womb she'd been waiting for the advent of Plaid Cymru[30]: she and my father, whom she had cured of his Lloyd George[31] Liberalism, were among the few hundred who voted for Lewis Valentine. Both would have been delighted with the eleven thousand votes received by Robyn Lewis[32] this year, just as I was.

We were given singing lessons by Mr Ellis – there was the sound of caps being lifted in the way we uttered his name. From somewhere between his windpipe and his nose came 'doh me soh doh – take the note, boys,' and then we would sail through 'In the paradise of Jesus / There are many homes of light / And they shine beyond the darkness / With a radiance clear and bright', or even '*Y Saith Rhyfeddod*' or '*Yn berl yng nghoron Iesu / Dymunwn Arglwydd fod*' – which was the standby just in case one of the pupils died. That happened twice while I was at the school. We, or at least I, would belt out the strangest things in English. Coming back to school after lunch-break, we sang a hymn. I don't recall anyone teaching us the words; we were assumed to have inherited them from our elders. Clearly, their transmission from generation to generation had played tricks with the original words, for what we sang was: '*We sant ti rod / Dy ryd da rwd.*' It was years later I learned that the intention of the grateful poet had been 'We thank thee, Lord, for this our food'.

At Penfforddelen we knew how to spell every difficult English word. This is how it was done. Mr Ellis was holding forth. 'I was coming along my garden path when something stuck in my throat.' Then he would make a noise like a frustrated waterfall deep in his throat, spit out the imaginary blockage and present us with a brandnew word 'I chwist it out – spell it.' And with one voice the class would shout, 'P-H-L-E-G-M. Phlegm.'

The aim of education was to pass the Scholarship, and this, too, was inevitable like the rising and setting of the sun, as far as we were concerned. There was no talk of the harmful psychological effects on young and vulnerable minds. I don't recall that I or my parents ever lost sleep over it. Nor do I know any contemporary of mine who found himself in middle age a half-crazed wretch in a madhouse on account of irresponsible loads being placed on weak backs. It wasn't that there was no will to succeed, for a pupil had to be one of the first twelve on the list to be given a free place at the Secondary School in Pen-y-groes. The teacher was Mr W.O. Jones, or Penbryn-bach as my mother called him because that was where he lived, one of the most devoted and stimulating teachers I ever had. He would write sample essays for us and we would learn them by heart. The title of one was 'A Typical Welsh farmer'. I still cherish a copy-book which contains all the exercises for the Scholarship. Hundreds of sums, most with an ostentatious R (for Right) against them. The written work is all in English. What surprises me is that at the age of ten, thanks to Mam, I was able to write quite neat and correct English. Here is an example: 'Late in the evening the poet reached home. He had been to a concert and had been enchanted by the admirable playing of a famous violin-player whom he had heard there.' But stranger still, I couldn't for the life of me speak the language. When, after five years in the County School, I'd entered University College, Bangor, if I happened to see someone coming with whom I'd have to speak English, I would make myself scarce through the first available exit.

One discipline which had to be mastered was parsing, or analysis, as we called it. Here is one example and not the most difficult either: 'We cannot kindle when we will the fire which in the heart resides.'[33] Years later, while I was trying to teach English in Pwllheli, I had a heated argument with one of His Majesty's Inspectors who objected to this kind of exercise. But not only was the ability of Welsh children to answer a whole exam question correctly worth taking trouble over for its own sake, but, for me, the knowledge of how a sentence is formed is the key to being able to write one neatly and with pleasure, too. In *Llais Llyfrau*[34] for Summer 1970 T.Wilson Evans said that he had recently listened to a talk dealing with words, clauses, sentences, paragraphs and writing in general. I have a feeling that I was the speaker. He goes on, 'And these were set out as if they were the essentials of great literature'. Mr Evans couldn't have been listening very carefully, for I'm certain that I said no such thing. What I am sure about is that every great writer is extremely careful of the way in which he expresses himself, that the shape of his sentences is deliberately designed to fit closely with their meaning. One has only to observe the sleepy sleekness of the opening sentences of *Cwrs y Byd*[35] and how they are followed by lively and vigorous writing to prove the point.

Looking at the copybook, I see that my spelling regularly let me down. Over and over again I had to write out words like 'quickly' (I left out the c) and 'unconscious' (the c again) and 'Wednesday' (no d). This brings to mind the first sentence in the passage given as dictation in the Scholarship exam: 'The lieutenant threw down his knapsack'. Although Mrs Prytherch, who was reading it aloud, said out of pity I like to think, 'liwtenant' and hinted at the k in 'knapsack', I hate to think what I wrote down.

Anyway, I managed to get into the first twelve and thus saved my parents from having to pay for my schooling – it was hard for a family who had to live on the scant wages of a stonemason, with not a penny coming in whenever it was wet and he was laid off work. The headmaster of the Pen-y-groes Intermediate School was Mr D.R.O. Prytherch (we called him Drop among ourselves, of course, or else Donkey Rider of Pen-y-groes). He was a mathematician, a Wrangler,[36] a fluent Welsh-speaker on Sundays in the big seat of the Independents' chapel, though I don't recall hearing a word of Welsh from his lips. The most important things I remember about him is that he stood with his back to the class while he solved problems on the blackboard, all the while calling out, 'D'you follow?' over his shoulder, and that the word 'talkative' was written in his italic hand on almost all my school reports. I can hear him this minute shouting 'Bend down!' before laying into some obedient and terrified wretch of a boy. And yet I have nothing against him personally.

The teacher who caused the greatest shiver to run down our spines was Mr Linton, a monoglot Englishman, a teacher without peer, with a permanently running nose, a tall and slim man. His nickname *Main* (Skinny) suited him perfectly. His subject was Science, something of which I'd never heard. There never was such a martinet of a disciplinarian. Not one of us dared misbehave in his class. If he hurled a duster, which he often did, and the dusters were hard-backed at Pen-y-groes, he hurled them with the intention of hitting his target and not for effect. The first question put to us in our very first class was 'Can you name a number less than nought?' That was how we were inducted into the mysteries of the word 'minus'. I could write a whole book about Linton.

It was he, without my realizing it at the time, of course, who made me understand that we are all, in a complex way, both comic and tragic creatures, with contradictory attributes running like twisted threads through the marrow of our bones. He had two, if not three daughters, but no son. One day his wife bore him a son. He didn't hurl a duster that day. He almost smiled in class. But about two days later the child died and, without his knowing, I saw Linton weeping in the corridor. What should we make of something like that? When my grandmother was ill I had to walk from Llandwrog the four miles to school every day. One day Linton came to the house with Dr Edwin, a great friend of his. I remember his saying to my mother, 'He has to walk all this distance every day then? Poor boy.' He was later appointed to the headship of the Secondary School in Newport in Monmouthshire. On his way there, he happened to get into the same compartment as me in the train from Pen-y-groes to Groeslon – it must have been raining to justify my going by train. He was shaking like a leaf, but he spoke to me very kindly, and before I got off at Groeslon he took me by the hand. 'I hope, Groeslon,' he said (he always called me Groeslon), 'I hope, Groeslon, that you'll do very well in your Senior.' Years later Tomos went to see him in Newport, an old man who had suffered a stroke. He could recall nothing of Pen-y-groes. But I shall remember him as someone who made a deep impression on me.

There was also Alexander Parry, the Latin master, with his little book into which he wrote your name with the warning, 'See me at four o'clock'. An honest, industrious and likeable teacher when you got to know him.

The teacher who taught English, Welsh and Geology was Mr David Davies, another Independent. You might have thought that being an Independent was a condition of appointment at Pen-y-groes. He was a stout, sleek man, not the most industrious of teachers by a long way, but the most effective reader I have ever heard. From him I first heard *Sioned*, though he was at his best when reading *Ivanhoe* and *The Lady of the Lake* and

Macbeth,[37] in a Welsh accent you could cut with a knife. I have since heard several actors playing Macbeth, including Lewis Casson, Redgrave, Olivier, Sybil Thorndyke and, last Sunday evening, Eric Porter and Janet Suzman, but give me Mr Davies every time:

> Glamis thou art and Cawdor and shalt be
> What thou art promised; yet do I fear thy nature;
> It is too full o' the milk of human kindness
> To catch the nearest way; thou wouldst be great,
> Art not without ambition, but without
> The illness should attend it.

And amid stifled bawdy laughter:

> Come to my woman's breasts
> And take my milk for gall, you murdering ministers.

I was close to tears when he declaimed:

> Wake Duncan with thy knocking! I wouldst thou couldst.

My debt to Mr Davies is great because he made me feel the thrill of literature.

But my debt is greater to Miss P.K.Owen, who came to the school to teach Welsh and made me feel the thrill of literature in my own language. To my great shame, I have only a hazy recollection of what we studied. Lots of Grammar – and in those days there was great emphasis on the Infixed Pronoun and the Pluperfect Tense – *Y Môr Canoldir a'r Aifft*, some of *Y Bardd Cwsg*, '*Cywydd y farn fawr*' and *Telenygion Maes a Môr*.[38] But Miss Owen's greatness lay not in what she taught us but in her own person. She was a fluent Welsh-speaker from Caernarfon, always spoke to us in good colloquial Welsh, knew Auntie Jane, Cefnrhengwrt, asked after my mother, treated everyone as an individual and proved it was possible to live a full life in the language that flowed naturally from our lips, much rougher perhaps than the correct English we wrote in our exercise books but warm and expressive, relaxed and comfortable. It was Miss Owen, with her firm conviction that true education means that you create something for yourself rather than regurgitate facts, who first asked us to write a play. She took mine to Gwynfor to be read. I still have the play; it makes me blush now but I shall never throw it in the fire. Miss Owen is still sprightly and dear to me. The price I pay for the help I received from her at school is that I kiss her whenever we meet.

From Pen-y-groes I went as a pupil-teacher to Pennforddelen at twenty pounds a year. I don't recall much about the teaching, but I do remember the kindness of Griff and Lily Jones who were teachers there; I also remember being given a ticket costing seven and sixpence – a small fortune in those days – by Gwilym Evans, the headmaster, to go and hear Leila Megane[39] singing at Soar chapel in Pen-y-groes. Her rendering of '*Cwsg fy anwylyd dinam / Tecach na'r rhosyn wyt ti*' haunted me day and night for weeks thereafter. It was about this time, too, I started playing tennis, the only game I have ever been any good at. We played on the schoolyard, the ball bouncing at whim so that when I later came to play on a comparatively flat court my racket often failed to make contact with the ball.

Then to College in Bangor – and Bangor in those days was as far from Groeslon as California. Tomos and I took digs with a Mr and Mrs Woodings and their widowed daughter, Mrs Jacobs, at 17 Park Street, in the back room. I found it difficult to relax there and we were often overcome with fits of laughter. Strange things happened in that house. Every morning Mr Woodings would collect our shoes for cleaning. 'Hello, Lord Carmel! Hello, Sir John!' Not that we had ever called ourselves that, though that's exactly how we felt. To crown the first night of term, Tom Madog Jones, the Students' President, called on us. In fact, he'd come to see his friends in the front room and had just looked in at the back to find out what lay in store for the College. It was an auspicious start to a very promising career. As everyone knows, Tomos was to have a distinguished one, while mine turned out to be quite ordinary.

Next morning we went to register. Up to now, my name had been John William Jones. I wrote it neatly on my form, which I took to Ifor Williams,[40] the Professor of Welsh. He knew my father – they had been at school together in Clynnog – and he used to come to tea at our house whenever he was preaching at

Brynrhos. 'Look,' he said, 'you'll have to change your name. There's another John William Jones, who registered before you. There's sure to be a lot of confusion. Hang on, William in Welsh is Gwilym. Call yourself John Gwilym Jones.' And so I was rechristened. It took months, no, years, before I grew used to my new name. I still warn people who want to leave me money in their wills what my real name is.

As I said, my academic career was very ordinary. I lacked the personality, obviously, to justify my becoming a member of any club or committee. Tomos immediately joined the famous Thirty Club and the Students' Council, and ended up Student President, though he didn't take up the post because he was appointed lecturer in Cardiff. I wasn't even a member of the select Welsh Club which had just been started. I won't deny that things like that used to hurt me and that I had pangs of disappointment, tears even. Living on the periphery of the exciting centre in which your closest friends move, though free from any responsibility, wasn't pleasant for a thin-skinned little creature like me. Not that I didn't know exactly what went on at even the most exclusive meetings. Tomos knew me well enough, and I him, to be able to tell each other everything. The gossip between us is just as unrestricted today as it ever was.

But there were meetings such as the Choir which everyone could attend. I was a keen enough member to get myself elected to the committee once, and this was so unusual that it inspired an *englyn*, a joint effort by Tomos, Meirion Roberts and Roger Hughes:

> *Y coryn ar bwyllgor Choral – bererin*
> *Diberoriaeth gwamal;*
> *Llais dylluan o'r anial*
> *Wna'r côr yn sobor o sâl.*

(The little chap on the Choir's committee – a pilgrim of shaky melody; an owl's voice from the wilderness will make the choir terribly poor.)

Then there was the Tair G,[41] the seed from which Plaid Cymru grew and of which I was for a while the secretary. But what more than anything saved me from total obscurity and encouraged the crumb of confidence in me was the Welsh Drama Society, with its genius of a producer, J.J. Williams, headmaster of Cefnfaes at Bethesda at the time. It was splendid to be allowed to sit open-mouthed and watch him working out significant moves, coaxing his actors to pronounce their lines clearly and deliver them effectively. The only snag was that I sat there as an observer. I was never given a part, not even an audition for a part. That used to make me cross because I often felt I could do much better than those who were chosen. I remember him producing *Y Ddraenen Wen* and *Gwyntoedd Croesion*[42] but the great play which, with no exaggeration, could be said to have given direction to drama in Wales was *Ty Dol*, Ifor Williams's translation of Ibsen's *A Doll's House*.[43] I shall never forget the search for a Nora. The casting of male actors was fairly easy, but I heard dozens reading her part. 'No,' J. J. would say in his somewhat nasal voice and draping his long body over an armchair and looking down his bespectacled nose at the points of his shoes. 'I know there's a Nora in this College, you see. I just know there is. And we must find her.' And in the end she was found – Elsie Evans from Llanystumdwy, who gave an intelligent and exciting performance. In saying, 'There's a Nora in this college, and she must be found,' J.J. was saying, in his subconscious, 'There's a wife for me in this College. And she must be found.' Soon afterwards he married Elsie.

I got a very ordinary degree, in Welsh and Economics of all things. Today I can remember none of the jargon of Economics except 'The Law of Diminishing Utility'. I was given two references, one by Professor Archer,[44] Daddy Archer, and the other by Ifor Williams. According to Archer, I was 'a very lively and stimulating teacher with a nice sense of humour', and according to Ifor Williams, 'To him as secretary (a job I was given because someone else had proved incompetent), more than to anyone, must be attributed the success of *Ty Dol*.' Both were exaggerations, I won't deny that, but the testimonials brought me comfort and satisfaction. One gave me confidence and the other am aim in life.

I got a teacher's job in London. In those days London agents used to interview applicants for jobs. 'Why do you wish to come to London?' asked one. 'Because,' I replied, 'I'm very fond of the theatre and teachers are better paid in London than anywhere else.' 'And we,' he replied with a grin, 'like to import people with a Welsh accent.' Anyway, whether on account of my shameless honesty or my accent, I got a job. And I enjoyed every minute of it for almost four years. I went to the theatre at least once a week – a seat in the gods cost only a few pence in those days. After two years William Vaughan Jones from Waun-fawr came to teach in the same school as me. I already knew him vaguely and today his home, Hafod y Coed, and that of his wife Mary, is a second home to me. In the same digs as Wil was J.E. Jones.[45] We were an inseparable trio and, when O.M. Roberts joined us, a foursome. We worked quite hard and conscientiously by day, but harder, if less conscientiously, by night and at weekends. Ping-pong, tennis, literary meetings in Charing Cross, the pillars of the cause on Sunday, and sometimes a trip to Box Hill,[46] Arsenal, the dirt-track, Wimbledon – a full, unadventurous, and entirely innocent life, it's true, but we were able to say each day, 'What a blessed life is this', despite the fact that often we didn't have a penny with which to look it in the face. J.E. has gone first, the most practically committed of us all – that's doubtless why.

I am very fond of music. I heard Kreisler[47] playing Bach's Chaconne unaccompanied at the Albert Hall and I used to go regularly to the old Queen's Hall where Henry Wood's Proms[48] were performed. I remember being thrilled by Beecham[49] galloping through the *Messiah* and I heard Menuhin play when he was a child prodigy. I would usually go to concerts on my own but we went to the theatre together. Going to see a play always gave me a brandnew thrill. We stood for hours in the queue, paid no attention to others as we rushed in to get a good seat, held our breath during the seconds of darkness before the curtain went up, and then suspended our disbelief as we watched Sybil Thorndyke, Edith Evans, John Gielgud, Edna Best, Godfrey Tearle, Miles Malleson, Cedric Hardwick – dozens and dozens of them. Last Saturday, on my way home from the continent, I saw three plays, no, four: *The Plebians* at half-past two at the Aldwych: David Storey's *Home* with John Gielgud and Ralph Richardson at the Apollo at five o'clock, and Pinter's *The Tea Party* and *The Basement* with Donald Pleasance and Vivienne Marchant at the Duchess at half-past eight. I was glad that I still got the thrill of anticipation before the curtain went up. Indeed, I'd go as far as to say that I more or less judge a man's character by his fondness for the theatre. My first question to anyone who's been to London is 'What did you see?', and I don't mean Westminster Abbey or Buckingham Palace. I'm often surprised by those who claim a love for the theatre when they say 'Nothing', or, worse, some dreadful musical or the Palladium.

My father and mother were always on about my coming to live nearer home, and somewhere in my subconscious my conscience accused me of being a traitor, reminding me that my place was in Wales, suffering adversity with God's own people, rather than taking endless pleasure in sin! Nowadays I'm very glad the faint pricking of conscience won the day, despite the fact that Wil Vaughan remembers my writing him a letter after being about a week in Llandudno, where I'd got a job in 1930, saying I was seriously considering chucking myself off the end of the pier. I stayed there for fourteen happy years in the end, living contentedly at the school with Humphrey Evans and Ffowc Williams, finding great pleasure in the Llandudno Welsh Drama Company and enjoying the hospitality and generous company of many new friends. One thing I learned there was that one had to be very angry with justices of the peace who, opiniated and ignorant, berate teachers when illiterate children are brought before them. I am absolutely convinced that there are some unfortunate little wretches with whom even the most committed, ingenious, conscientious and sympathetic teacher can do nothing. The same facilities for everyone, by all means, but how the heck do some of the theoreticians who have never stood in front of a class not see that not everyone can make the same use of the facilities?

It was a most fortunate day for me when I was appointed to a teaching post at the Pwllheli County School in 1944. The standard of the children's intelligence there was much higher, their behaviour civilized in a country sort of way, and the school's discipline quietly firm under its Headmaster, R.E. Hughes, a courteous man, of beautiful common sense and a Welshman by conviction. I liked the town, too. I was able to ask everyone how they were and always got a civil reply. It was only a sudden whim that took me from there to Pen-y-groes, my old school, four years later. I was then able to live at home, of course, and found it easy to deal with everyone at school, and yet I was still restless and when I applied for a job with the BBC in the year following, I got it. I began as a talks producer and became a producer of plays. The novelty of the work was exciting at first, but as I got used to it I had to admit that I was still restless. I missed the routine of starting at nine in the morning and finishing at four, and, on the quiet, the long holidays. I also had to face the fact that I wasn't, by nature, intended to deal with adults – I understood children and young people better. But more than anything I could not rid myself of the feeling that I was wasting my time. I had to read scores of plays that were, to me at least, completely hopeless, and then to write politely explaining why they'd been turned down, and by so doing I inevitably caused bad feeling. Some argue that a man isn't worth his salt if he has no enemies. Perhaps so, but I'm quite content, if possible, to be unworthy of my salt where literature is concerned. Politics are another matter. And then, after choosing a play for broadcasting and finding suitable actors, there were three days of crazy rehearsals and, during the performance, despite the cry of 'Don't panic' on all sides, I sweated gallons. For what? Just to read a line or two of patronizing praise or ignorant condemnation in the Welsh or English press – there was no distinction between them. That was the end of it. For me, because I was used to seeing some permanent result for my labours – children passing an exam, and I'm enough of a Tory to see nothing wrong in examinations, the children thanking me for being able to cast light on something that had been perplexing them, or children so delighted with poetry that it became their life's pleasure – the transience of my work at the BBC was a daily frustration for me.

There then occurred a fateful coincidence. In 1953 I was invited to address the Rotary Club in Bangor and I chose the topic 'Words'. The chairman was Sir Emrys Evans,[50] the Principal of the College. Shortly after the publication of my book *Y Goeden Eirin* in 1946, he'd written me a letter which is among the few I have ever kept. Shortly after speaking to the Rotary, I called on Tomos and Enid Parry and during our chat I expressed my unease at my lot. That was all. A few days later Tomos rang asking me to come and see him. By this time he'd been appointed National Librarian and was about to leave Bangor for

Aberystwyth. 'Would you like to come to the College as a lecturer?' he asked. Only once had I fainted and this was almost the second time. Then I was told that Sir Emrys had mentioned my Rotary talk and would like to see me. To cut a long story short, I was appointed and was quite sure that I lived in the second age of miracles. There I was, with no qualifications of any importance, not a scholar of any kind, getting a job which several others in Wales, academics and scholars, at least, deserved much more. Some, moreover, were not slow in saying so privately and in the public prints. I couldn't blame them. Anyway, I comfort myself that T. Gwynn Jones[51] had been my distinguished predecessor, and the thrill of it was enough to smother whatever shame or guilt might trouble me. I shall be retiring, if I am still alive, next year, after eighteen years at the College, having enjoyed not just every minute but every second of them.

This talk was first broadcast in two parts by BBC Cymru in the radio series *Y Llwybrau Gynt* in 1971 and published in *Atgofion* (*Ty ar y Graig*, 1972), together with scripts by Kate Roberts, Thomas Parry and William Morris.

Afterword

John Gwilym Jones was born on 27 September 1904 at 6 Rathbone Terrace, Y Groeslon, a village situated about six miles from Caernarfon in north Wales. He lived for the greater part of his life at Angorfa in this village. Y Groeslon was, and still is to a great extent, Welsh in speech and attitudes. In John Gwilym's boyhood and youth this was an agricultural and a slate-quarrying area. Like most parts of Wales at the beginning of the last century it was, in religion, strongly Nonconformist. He was the only child of Griffith Thomas Jones, a stonemason, and Jane Jones.

He was born into a society that had a high regard for education, though in a rather narrow way – a large number of those educated to the higher forms of secondary schools and colleges became ministers of religion or teachers. John Gwilym attended the local elementary school, Penfforddelen, from 1908 to 1916, and Penygroes Grammar School from 1916 to 1921. He spent the year 1921-22 as what was called a 'pupil teacher', before proceeding to the University College of North Wales, Bangor, where he remained from 1922 to 1926. It is worth noting that until registration day at university, John's name was John William Jones; the Gwilym instead of William was suggested by Professor Ifor Williams, head of the Welsh Department, because another John William Jones had already registered – this to avoid confusion. One of his fellow-students, at school and university, was John's lifelong friend Thomas Parry, sometime Professor of Welsh at Bangor, and later Head of the National Library of Wales, and then Principal of the University College of Wales, Aberystwyth.

John Gwilym became a teacher and served at Millfields Road Elementary School, Clapton, London (1926-30), and then at the following schools in north Wales: the Central School, Llandudno (1930-44), Pwllheli Grammar School (1944-48), and Penygroes Grammar School (1948-49). In 1949 he was appointed Director of Drama with the BBC in Wales at Bangor. In 1953 he was appointed Lecturer in the Department of Welsh at the University College of North Wales, Bangor. He took a prominent part in the teaching and the production of drama throughout his time at the

University. He remained in the Department until his retirement in 1971, having been promoted Reader. In 1973 he was awarded an honorary DLitt. He died, suddenly, whilst re-opening a chapel vestry in Y Groeslon on 16 October, 1988. His cremated ashes were buried in his parents' grave at Llandwrog five days later.

In an article entitled 'A Word from a Friend' in a volume published in John's honour, Sir Thomas Parry refers to his development into "a multifaceted character" from "a not very colourful little boy." John himself has admitted to being a fearful boy, not keen on keeping company with any gang of boys, and happiest left to his own devices at his grandmother's in Caedoctor, not far from his home. Thomas Parry, who in later life was a powerful and determined character, unexpectedly says that he was not unlike him. He refers to the shyness bred into his generation and, significantly, suggests that it may have had something to do with their education, of being greeted and guided in English, a language that they only half understood, without having the opportunity of expressing their thoughts orally in that language, or their own language – expressing themselves on paper in English or Welsh was another matter altogether. John himself refers to the speaking of English:

> I couldn't for the life of me speak the language. When, after five years in the County School I'd entered University College, Bangor, if I happened to see someone coming with whom I'd have to speak English, I would make myself scarce through the first available exit.

Later on, especially after his years in London, things changed, but I can recall even when he was on the staff of the Welsh Department in Bangor that he felt rather apprehensive when he had to address a combined meeting of the Welsh and English Literary Societies in English. As a matter of record, he was by far the best speaker at that meeting, but this apprehensiveness was deep-seated. It is something that is beyond the understanding of most English-speakers and, until recently, the English legal system.

The plum tree at his grandmother's house in Caedoctor is the Plum Tree in the story, though used there for a particular

purpose. The grandmother appears in some detail in John's play
Ac Eto nid Myfi (And yet, not I). Those who know that play will
pick up other details from John's life, such as the main character's love of onions – see "They [onions] made my mouth water,
and still do" in 'The Man from Groeslon'. John's mother, in one
form or another, appears in the same play and in several other
works by him. His preoccupation with family and family ties are
based on his own experience of family life, though there are, of
course, imaginative variations on this experience. John's friendship with Thomas Parry may well have been the basis of Huw
and Wil's friendship in *Ac Eto nid Myfi*. 'Families' and 'friends'
figure prominently in his works, and they are the themes that
give expression to words that seem to convey John's deepest
convictions – as, for example, the words at the end of the play
Hanes Rhyw Gymro (The Story of a Certain Welshman) where
Morgan Llwyd, an eminent divine, preacher, writer and
Parliamentarian in the seventeenth century who, in John's play,
turned to various forms of Christian beliefs and creeds before,
finally, facing his own truth about the only certainty in this life,
of love between a man and his family and his friends. At the end
of the play Morgan is with his family and takes his baby in his
arms and sings a lullaby, the lullaby that his friend Siencyn,
whose request for the sign of the cross he had refused when he
was dying, once sang to his child. In *Y Tad a'r Mab* (The Father
and the Son), a title with a telling absence of any mention of the
Holy Ghost, a father's attitude to his gifted son ends in tragedy
on a Biblical scale. In John's pre-eminently Welsh world, though
most decidedly a sophisticated Welsh world, there are sometimes
hints and murmurs of emotions that would not be out of place
in a Greek tragedy, or in stories from the Old Testament..

I have already referred to the strong Nonconformism of the
time of John's childhood. In comparing life today and life when
he was a child John has this to say:

> It was a time of unquestioning acceptance with no sense that
> a man's freedom was being impinged upon or his personal-
> ity impaired... In essence they [people in general] accepted
> the status quo as being eternally right.

He goes on to recall his heroically regular presence in various chapel meetings, but notes that his contrariness meant that he detested it. For anyone living in the 'anything goes' liberality of today it is almost impossible to realise how difficult it would have been for John to face up to his own lack of belief in the supernatural basics of Nonconformist Christianity, but he did so. Yet he still attended his chapel, and still played the organ there from time to time – occasionally telling ex-student preachers that he could not 'play that hymn-tune' and could they lead another hymn please. His sometime minister used to say that his grasp of the practicalities of the Christian religion was so high that it was no wonder that he classed himself as a non-believer. But beliefs pressed upon us in childhood are not easily put aside, and I remember him telling me, after he had recovered from a near-fatal car accident in America – in which he had been passenger – that he had no memory at all of several hours after the collision; he had no glimpse of any other world, so death was the end. "But John, I thought you already believed that," I said. His words were, "Yes, but..."

In any case, if he wanted to portray the life of Welsh people in his kind of society, then religion would have to be a part of their lives. There are frequent echoes of or references to the translation of the Welsh Bible of William Morgan (1588), the rich tradition of Welsh hymns, and the formulaic utterances of worshippers in the *Seiat* [Fellowship] or prayer meetings in his plays and prose. These were an integral part of the community he knew so well, especially the community of his earlier work. But it was a community with its beliefs in decline, and John examines the beliefs of his characters with a penetrating gaze. Here is the minister in 'The Wedding':

> I move between the bickering deacons and the death-rattle of my flock... Weaned of the ambition of youth, its visions and hopes and joys, I grew into the lukewarm, quotidean ordinariness of a good minister of Jesus Christ, and became content with my lot.

In 'Meurig' the portrayal of the 'religious' father is low-key dismemberment:

> He spoke gently, sympathetically, in the voice he kept for

funerals and other emotional occasions to do with the Ministry such as denouncing a drunkard or expelling someone from the Fellowship meeting.

In 'The Communion' he evokes the joy of a passionate believer:

He observed Dyffrin Ysig from one cleft to another, across its smooth blue bed and its wooded sides, and he beheld the kingdom of heaven. He turned the aftergrass and the new corn as work given him from the right hand of God. In the bubbling of the small brooks which lose themselves in the water of the Ysig he heard the Song of Moses and the Song of the Lamb. The trees clapped their hands and chanted to him as they dropped their myriad green leaves. The Son of Man walked upon the stone walls and intensified the colours of the flowers and quickened the songs of robin and wren. He was at home.

There are no Taffies in John's work. He detested with a ferocity that belied his timid childhood anything with a whiff of Taffydom in it – his stand on behalf of the Welsh language and Wales were also always strikingly fearless. For John, Taffydom is the servile representation of the Welsh, mainly by Welsh men, for the entertainment of the English. They appear as 'look yous' and as hypocrite chapel-goers, or as rude, idiosyncratic peasants of low cunning. They are the ones that populate the writings of Caradoc Evans – according to John – and Dylan Thomas's *Under Milk Wood* was not much better. In the same congregation were the anti-Welsh-language Labour politicians of south Wales – or north Wales, for that matter. According to John, not only were such people not Welsh but they were anti-Welsh, bent on destroying his nation: as he put it, "Language and nation are synonymous". But Labour politicians of the past may be comforted to know that on a Richter scale of animosity they did not register when compared to John's attitude to Margaret Thatcher! One of his fond sayings at election time, whether they were parliamentary or local government elections, was that many Labour voters would put their crosses for a chimpanzee. But he was honest enough to admit, with a laugh, that he himself had in one local government election voted for a chimpanzee – of the Plaid Cymru species. In his own writings, the characters are mostly intelligent and well-read, some of them very well-read, in Welsh, English, European and American literature; and it is not unusual for them to be people of wide culture, with an enlightened interest in classical music. In his plays, this acceptance of intelligence may have been an antidote to Welsh 'back-kitchen dramas' (*dramâu cegin gefn*) that were such a strong feature of amateur theatre in Wales, especially during the first half of the twentieth century. Many of his characters are endowed with John's own intelligence and his own vast reading and the benefit of his theatre-going. This is one reason why Meic Stephens had his work cut out in annotating this selection of John's prose. In 'The Wedding' John Llywelyn Evans, the bridegroom, thinks that he would like to be a critic:

> ... and able to list the books of the ages in order of merit. That's not possible, of course. It would not be difficult to choose the books at either end. My large pipes [he compares the most important with the pipes of the chapel organ] would be the Bible and the Mabinogi. "Yes," my critics would say, "we are quite happy to have the Bible at one end, but why the Mabinogi? Have you not heard of Euripides and Tacitus and Shakespeare and Cervantes and Dante and Balzac and Tolstoy and Goethe and..?" "Of course I have, I've heard of them all, but I'm a Welshman." "Ah," they would say pedantically, "literature is above nationality. You mustn't think within the limits of your own country; you have to reach out, widen your horizons and see author and book in their proper place as part of a development of world literature; you must acquire a classical mind and learn how to compare and contrast and discover how much an author learned from those who went before him. Then decide whether he added anything or merely lived off the riches of his forebears. A good critic has to know where lyric and novel come from. They're not made of nothing, hovering in the air and unconnected as gossamer. It's mere romanticism to think like that, criticism that is nothing but personal taste or whim.

Any bridegroom who thought like this at his wedding must have been devoted to literature well beyond the call of duty, but what is said here is of great significance to anyone interested in John Gwilym Jones the Literary Critic. In his criticism there is a constant comparison of a particular work under consideration with other works of literature, other works of Welsh literature (in 'The Communion' he refers to the illegitimate child Meurig: "He had never known who his parents were. He was, like the contemporary literature of Wales, pitifully ignorant of his lineage"), and other works from Western literature – the comparisons are almost always on a grand scale. Welsh literature, especially, must be seen to be able to bear such comparisons. Also in his criticism there is regular defining of genre, or of literature in general. Dafydd Glyn Jones has gone as far as to say that, as a critic, his main interest is in exploring 'What is literature?' John Gwilym Jones is intensely interested in how literature works, and his constant referene to this work or that has nothing to do with displaying the extent of his own reading and everything to do with his passion for analysis, an analysis which enriches his own writing. As he says in the paragraph quoted, works of literature are not made of nothing. There is such a thing as the limit, the cutting edge in creative writing, as in scientific search. Any critic worthy of the name has some idea where this limit is, and what works advance that limit. These are the *avant garde* of literature. Whether works of the *avant garde* have any real worth, only time will tell, and only time will tell whether works that once appeared new or 'experimental', as the saying goes, have any distinction. (In recent times, in fine art as in literature, experimentalism seems to have become an end in itself, as if newness at all costs were the sole criterion of achievement.) But real newness and real worth will be revealed, even if works of such newness may be reviled at the time of composition. That is what happened with James Joyce's *Ulysses*, for example.

It is pertinent to refer to *Ulysses*, for that is one work that has an obvious and positive influence on John's collection of stories, *Y Goedin Eirin*. The 'stream of consciousness' – old hat by now – was, in Joyce's work, revolutionary. In Welsh, John's book was also revolutionary – he brought into the language a new way of writing. There are sections of *Ulysses* where the minds, emotions and recollections of the characters wander hither and thither suggesting, but not actually conveying, the stream of their consciousness – that would be an impossible task. John Gwilym Jones's 'The Wedding' and 'The Highest Cairn', especially, are examples of 'stream of consciousness' writing, though it is more highly regulated than in Joyce. If there is any specific example of *Ulysses'* influence on John's work it is the one quoted below. At the end of the first chapter of *Ulysses* Stephen Dedalus looks for his handkerchief:

> My handkerchief. He threw it. I remember. Did I not take it up?
> His hands groped vainly in his pockets. No, I didn't. Better buy one.
> He laid the dry snot picked from his nostril on a ledge of rock, carefully. For the rest let look who will.

In 'The Highest Cairn' the prisoner, whilst talking to a minister, remembers things from his past:

> Don't pick your nose, Mam used to say. But later I made a fine art of picking it. I knew precisely when a snot was ready to be plucked out with a finger-nail. I would dislodge it in one fell swoop. And Oh, the lovely feeling of rolling it into a ball between finger and thumb before disposing of it.

Some of the unappetizing details of life are recorded in both works. And if you find this description unpleasant, you should try Leopold Bloom's thoughts on defecation, whilst seated on a lavatory pan in *Ulysses*. But although Joyce had an influence on John's work, the total effect of the writing in this book and in *Ulysses* are altogether different. John's work is imbued with a Welsh, Nonconformist consciousness; Joyce's work is Irish and Catholic, not to say Jesuitical – even though he turned his back on all of that, or tried to.

In a way, Enid, in 'The Stepping Stones', passes judgement on John's work (John seems to be the Absalom in the story, and Tomos may well be Thomas Parry, and Enid, his wife):

> I'm fed up with these stories without a structure, that presuppose an idea and Freudian analysis are sufficient to create literature.

She sees people doing things.
But what Absalom sees are people living, moving and being

inside themselves. He adds, in his own defence:

> I don't see why I have to devise credible circumstances.
> What's important is to see that the characters' response to
> their circumstances, whether credible or not, is a true, full
> and fair one.

From the point of view of John's writing these words are of great importance as, indeed, is the whole story from which they are taken.

Dr Enid Roberts, a distinguished colleague of John in the Welsh Department at Bangor, used to quote one of his regular sayings with amusement. John would declare, raising his right arm for emphasis, "I'm absolutely certain," adding, in the same breath with the fall of this same arm, "more or less." – "*Dwi'n hollol sicir, fwy neu lai*". This is one key phrase that reveals a great deal about John's work and his character. Another key phrase about him is Thomas Parry's:

> [here's a man whose] clothes are strikingly neat and trim, but
> who is never sure in what pocket he has his money or his car
> keys.

Any Welshman worth his salt works in Triads, so I add a third key phrase – a poor one, but mine own. One day John was by his front door when a passing neighbour stopped and asked him: "John, what's a nihilist?"

"Someone who doesn't believe, especially in religious creeds; someone who doesn't believe in anything," John answered. "Why?"

"Well, that's what you are."

It turned out that John been called "the nihilist from Y Groeslon" in a recent article in the Welsh weekly publication *Y Cymro* by the psychiatrist Gwilym O. Roberts. But if he was in one sense a nihilist, he was also one of the most creative human beings that anyone could hope to meet; hence my 'The Creative Nihilist from Y Groeslon'. All these phrases have one thing in common, they point out a paradox. A paradox, in this context, is a conflict of attitudes or a contradiction in the same person. There are several occasions when John makes the point that life is a paradox. He was fond of quoting William Blake's poem, 'The Sick Rose':

> O Rose, thou art sick!
> The invisible worm
> That flies in the night,
> In the howling storm
>
> Has found out thy bed
> Of crimson joy,
> And his dark secret love
> Does thy life destroy.

Beauty is infested; in love there is destruction. It is almost an article of faith with John that we should be made aware of the contraries in life. In 'The Highest Cairn' the prisoner thinks that the Welsh are unwilling to accept the contraries:

> But in Welsh the daisy is observed without the sheep's droppings, the sleek skin of the horned cattle without their dung, the baby's curls and cooing without the bleeding womb.

In 'The Plum Tree' Wil says:

> Good and bad, my boy, are so intermingled that you just can't draw a line between them...

In the part of the unfinished novel, 'Meurig', the main character goes out into the wild after his mother dies:

> It was April and the vigour of spring had brought out the blossom and lambs; wild strawberries, primroses and buttercups grew in clusters under the hedges. He picked a buttercup and put it under his chin to see whether the pollen would stick there. He noticed how shiny the petals were, like mucus, and suddenly they turned on him as if they were some horrible food. He crushed a primrose and observed the many black insects that swarmed tirelessly at the base of the petals. He was astonished at how many times he had smelt the scent of primroses. He imagined the black creatures making their way up his nose and down his throat and through his whole body. He threw away the flower and

> stamped it into the earth. A few steps further on he saw a
> wren's nest, the first of the year. His heart beat with joy and
> he immediately stuck his finger into it. He was nervous.
> There is danger in a wren's nest. There is no way of knowing
> what lurks in the darkness. A snake perhaps, the early
> warmth having woken it from hibernation.

This conviction of the duality of life sometimes appears as an interest in twins (as in the story 'The Plum Tree') and in a general preoccupation with doubles – a theme discussed with perceptive insight by Mihangel Morgan in a PhD thesis on John's work. Meurig and Gwyn in 'The Communion' are a case in point. The extreme point of the double is a kind of schizophrenia, as in Jeckyll and Hyde, but the duality need not reach that extreme; the more usual example is that of a couple who in some way complement each other.

John's preoccupation with duality leads on to another of what might almost be called his fixations, and that is hypocrisy. He often referred to a section of Daniel Owen's novel, *Rhys Lewis*, to support his belief that hypocrisy is the necessary 'oil of society'. In that novel Rhys Lewis confesses to a revered deacon, Abel Hughes, a lapse or sin that Daniel Owen chose not to reveal to his readers – thus making it more powerful because the readers will begin to imagine what it can be. The advice given to Rhys by Abel Hughes is:

> Don't tell anyone else: because, if this comes to men's ears,
> though God may forgive you, it may be held against you
> whilst you are alive.

We all live by not revealing aspects of ourselves. In one interview Marlon Brando declared that acting was not such a big deal. "We all act," he said. If a woman wears a new dress you may well tell her how beautiful her dress is, even though you may not think so at all. That is acting, so he said; and that is hypocrisy on a small scale, the kind which helps turn the wheels of society. In the selected prose of this book we see what is said and what is thought in 'The Wedding', the difference between the two is an example of the kind of hypocrisy that makes society possible. Thomas Lewis, Meurig's father (see 'Meurig') is a more sinister example of hypocrisy.

There is a great deal of attention, sensual attention, to 'things' in this book. That attention may generate enjoyment or disgust; or a combination of both (see the section above on duality). This is a feature in literature that John often referred to as a critic. There are many examples of sensual evocation in his own work:

> At his feet grew clump of groundnuts and on their tough tops there were greyish-white flowers, as big as a child's open palm. He took out his pocket-knife and cut around the stem of one. He dug until he could feel the tip of his finger under the nut and pulled it out carefully by its root. He cleaned it and enjoyed its dry brittleness between his teeth and the taste of earth on his tongue.

> He remembered the spring in Nant Cae Ffridd and the sticky buds bursting like sores and healing into pretty green leaves, the grey anemone like tuberculosis with its black and green serrations, the clumps of primroses, their fragrance drifting like an echo, a lonely daffodil illuminating the shade at the foot of a tree, the yellow flag and blue iris like thick-legged louts in the dampness, the Pant Rhedyn cattle straying and chewing the cud in the rushes, the water-wheel in the distance creaking on its axle.

> ... up to the Gwyllt with its strong beech-trees that are as pretty in winter as they are in spring, their bark the colour of lavender and shiny as brocaded silk.

In the Nonconformist world of John's childhood sex was a taboo subject in polite society. In practice, as we could say, it was otherwise:

> My mother had cousin who had run off to America – a paternity case, no doubt,

and in Evelyn Waugh's *Decline and Fall* Dr Fagan in his north Wales public school perceived, as early as 1928, that "we can trace almost all the disasters of English history to the influence of the Welsh", from Edward of Caernarfon, through the times of the Tudors and the dissolution of the Church to "Lloyd George, the temperance movement, Nonconformity, and lust stalking hand in hand through the country, wasting and ravaging". But in the world of John's childhood, parents were as likely to explain the details of sex to their children as explain the theory of relativity. Because of this there was more mystery and more of a frisson of sinfulness in it than nowadays when we have sex with everything. This is an area in John's work where Joyce had little influence, nor the rampant D.H. Lawrence, with whose work John was well-acquainted. The polite attitude to sex is revealed in '*Y Tad a'r Mab*' where Gwyn's parents never kiss openly ("*Welis i 'rioed nhad yn cusanu mam*" [I never saw my dad kiss my mam]). It is also revealed, perhaps more significantly, in the play *Dwy Ystafell* (Two Rooms) where Meic is supposed to be a Lothario but is, in fact, no more than a damp squib. A self-conscious shyness, and a sense of taboo remained with John more or less throughout his work. Or, perhaps one should say, that there are no sex extravaganzas in his work, none of the detailed descriptions of intimacy which are now two a penny ("I have not, like Anais Nin, written erotic books to pay for the upkeep of my children"). But a close scrutiny of the prose translated here throws up an occasional remarkable observation, one or two of them edging towards an openness that we now take for granted:

> I shall have bouts of lust without the forgiveness of lusting together, followed by drowsy, lonely torpor. And pain and guilt next morning; for I can never free myself from the chains of the Ten Commandments or the shackles of the thousand and one commandments of my own home.

> I am the sacred vessel preserved by Joseph of Arimathea. Here I am, in the court of Pelles, the grandfather of Galahad, in all the splendour of my holiness, pure, intact, like the Virgin Mary, undefiled, immaculate. Who comes now on a pilgrimage from Arthur's court at Camelot? Who is this with golden spurs on his right foot? Burt? Lionel? Percival? Galahad? Come, my Galahad! Come, O predestined seeker of the Holy Grail... Come, and I shall succour thee with my spiritual food, I shall show thee my secrets, I shall anoint thee king of my realm. Come! Come!

Afterword

> He came into physical contact with her and every touch was like a piercing flame to her maidenhood. One day he kissed her, and from that moment there was no doubt... Starved of the pleasures of the flesh for so long, they became everything to her... How lovely the urgency in the anticipation of passion, how exquisite the subsequent langour. She was like a healthy animal. Life returned to her dark eyes, colour to her cheeks and lips. Her black hair shone, she moved with nimble grace.

I think that anyone who knew John Gwilym Jones will acknowledge that there is a remarkable degree of oneness in his personality, his prose writing, his plays, and his criticism. In both his life and work there is an inveterate curiosity (he once said, paradoxically, that he would like a small window in the side of his coffin so that he could see how people behaved at his funeral), a keen observation of people and the world about us, a sense of the duality of things, a Christian morality that has separated itself from dogma, together with an intelligence that has inherited the literary aspect of that dogma in remarkable detail. His life and work convinced him that the most elemental thing in our sojourn in this world is the relationship between people.

GWYN THOMAS

Notes

These notes are intended to help the general reader to a better understanding of the author's work by throwing light on some of the many allusions in the texts, in particular references to Welsh, Biblical and literary matters.

The Craft of the Short Story

1. Saunders Lewis (1893-1985), playwright and literary critic, generally considered to be the greatest Welsh writer of the 20th century; see also 'The Communion', note 12; Kate Roberts (1891-1985), the most distinguished of all Welsh short-story writers; J.O Williams (1892-1973) wrote stories about the people of the quarrying districts of north-west Wales, and Islwyn Williams (1903-57) set his in the Swansea Valley.

2. Llandwrog, the native parish of John Gwilym Jones, is situated to the south of Caernarfon; the village of Groeslon, where the author was born and lived for many years, is on the A487.

3. See the story 'On the Mend'.

4. For the Maid of Cefn Ydfa see 'The Wedding', note 6.

5. For the Mabinogion and the Grail see 'The Wedding', notes 5 and 10.

6. Daniel Owen (1836-95), Welsh novelist; Dafydd ap Gwilym (fl.1315/20-1350/70), the greatest Welsh poet of the medieval period; for Ann Griffiths (1776-1805), hymn-writer, see 'The Wedding', note 11; Robert Williams Parry (1884-1956), poet; Llywarch Hen is the old man in an anonymous sequence of poems from the 9th or 10th century in which he laments the death in battle of his 24 sons; William Williams (1717-91) of Pantycelyn, hymn-writer.

7. See 'The Communion'.

8. For Dafydd ap Gwilym see note 6 above; Morgan Llwyd (1619-59), Puritan author of the prose masterpieces *Llythur ir Cymru Cariadus* ('A letter to the loving Welsh people'; 1653) and *Llyfr y Tri Aderyn* ('Book of the three birds'; 1653), see also 'On the Mend', note 5; Robert Williams Parry see note 6 above ; T.H. Parry-Williams (1887-1975), poet and essayist.

9. Virginia Woolf (1882-1941), English novelist; Ernest Hemingway (1899-61), William Saroyan (1908-81), and Sherwood Anderson (1876-1941), American novelists; Marcel Proust (1871-1922), French novelist; James Joyce (1882-1941), Irish novelist.

10. *Gweledigaethau y Bardd Cwsc* ('Visions of the sleeping bard'), a prose

masterpiece by the devotional writer Ellis Wynne (1671-1734); for *Llythur ir Cymru Cariadus* and *Llyfr y Tri Aderyn* see note 8 above.

11. Robert Louis Stevenson (1850-94), Scottish writer.
12. See 'The Stepping Stones'.
13. Admiral Horatio Nelson (1758-1805), at the battle of Copenhagen in 1803, was said to have put his telescope to his blind eye, thus making sure he did not see a signal ordering him to desist from action.
14. See 'The Man from Groeslon', note 24.

The Wedding

1. The reference is to Joseph Parry's opera, *Blodwen* (1878).
2. 'And the third day there was a marriage in Cana of Galilee; and the mother of Jesus was there.' (John, 2:1). It was at the wedding in Cana that Jesus performed the miracle of turning water into wine.
3. Ivan Petrovitch Pavlov (1849-1936), the Russian physiologist, studied conditioned reflexes in animals; in one experiment he caused dogs to salivate at the prospect of food by ringing a bell at certain times of day.
4. *Y Faner*, a weekly newspaper launched in 1859 by Thomas Gee (1815-98) as *Baner ac Amserau Cymru* (lit. 'The Flag and Times of Wales') was staunchly Liberal in outlook, defended Nonconformity against the Established Church and supported such Radical causes as Temperance, Home Rule and the Land Question. Between 1923 and his death the paper's editor was the poet E. Prosser Rhys (1901-45).
5. The first four of the twelve tales known in English as *The Mabinogion* are known in Welsh as *Pedair Cainc y Mabinogi* ('The Four Branches of the Mabinogi'), namely the stories of Pwyll, Branwen, Manawydan and Math. To these Lady Charlotte Guest (1812-95) added the tales of Culhwch and Olwen, Macsen Wledig, Lludd and Llefelys, Rhonabwy, Peredur, Owain, Geraint and Enid, and Taliesin, which she published as *The Mabinogion* between 1838 and 1849. The best modern translation of the tales, generally considered to be the major prose masterpiece of the medieval period, is that by Thomas Jones and Gwyn Jones, published in 1948.
6. The tragic heroine Ann Thomas (1704-27) was known as the Maid of Cefn Ydfa after her father's home near Llangynwyd in Glamorgan. At the age of twenty-one she is said to have married, against her will, a rich lawyer named Anthony Maddocks. She was in love, so the story goes, with Wil Hopcyn, a young poet, who composed the verses '*Bugeilio'r Gwenith Gwyn*' ('Watching the White Wheat') for her. Soon after marriage to Maddocks, Ann is reputed to have died of a broken heart. This romantic tale, which was encouraged by Iolo Morganwg (Edward

Williams;1747-1826), is now known to have had no basis in historical fact.

7. Clark Gable (1901-60), an American film actor, also starred in *Gone with the Wind* (1939).

8. The *Seiat* is known in English as the Fellowship; in Methodist chapels it was the occasion for prayer, Bible reading and the expression of spiritual experiences.

9. Sarras, in the legend of the Holy Grail, is the place to which Joseph of Arimathea flees from Jersusalem and where Galahad dies after seeing the ultimate mystery. Moradrins is the Welsh form of Mordrain, king of Sarras, whom Joseph of Arimathea helps to fight against his rival, Tholomer.

10. The Quest for the Holy Grail, believed to be part of the True Cross preserved by Joseph of Arimathea, is the subject of a number of medieval poems and prose works, notably that by Chrétien de Troyes (fl. 1170-90), in which Arthurian themes are prominently featured. Versions of the tale were popular in Wales. In Malory's *Le Morte d'Arthur* (c.1450), Galahad is the son of Launcelot and Elaine, daughter of King Pelles. He is predestined by his immaculate purity to find the Grail, after the vision of which he dies in ecstasy. Burt and Lionel are two of Arthur's knights.

11. Ann Griffiths (1776-1805) of Dolwar-fach in the parish of Llanfihangel-yng-ngwynfa, Montgomeryshire, was a hymn-writer in whose work some critics have discerned mystical qualities. Her main themes were the person and sacrifice of Jesus Christ, her love for Him, and her longing for sanctity and heaven. Her hymns are powerful expressions of her religious zeal and she is generally regarded as the finest of all Welsh hymn-writers.

The Plum Tree

1. *Taid* and *Nain* are the names used in North Wales for Grandfather and Grandmother respectively; in South Wales the names are *Tadcu* and *Mamgu*.

2. The reference is to the song '*Arafa Don*', the music for which was written by R.S. Hughes (1855-93).

3. The author is echoing the account of God's creation of the world in the Book of Genesis I.

4. Nebuchadnezzar was ruler of the Babylonian Empire from 605 BC until his death in 562. There are references to him in nine of the books in the Old Testament. In the Book of Daniel, a voice from heaven chas-

tises him for his pride as the builder of Babylon with the words: 'The kingdom is departed from thee. And they shall drive thee from men, and thy dwelling shall be with the beasts of the field: they shall make thee to eat grass as oxen...' (Daniel 4:31-32). This prophecy comes about immediately.

5. Daniel, a biblical hero whose deeds and prophecies are recorded in the Old Testament book that bears his name, was cast into a den of lions for continuing to pray to his own God while a captive in Babylon, but was divinely delivered. (Daniel, 6).

6. George Bernard Shaw (1856-1950), an Irish man of letters and free-thinker.

7. Joseph Stalin (born Dzhugashvili; 1879-1953), a Marxist revolutionary who in 1924 succeeded Lenin as leader of the Soviet Union, which he ruled with an iron fist until his death; he led the Soviets during the second world war.

8. William Ewart Gladstone (1809-98), English statesman, leader of the Liberal Party and Prime Minister four times between 1868 and 1894.

9. Evan Roberts (1878-1951), an evangelist, was the leader of a religious revival which swept through Wales in 1904-05.

10. Karl Barth (1886-1968), a German theologian and pastor. An opponent of National Socialism during the Nazi years, he was also a pacifist and the leading spirit behind the Barmen Declaration of 1934 which formulated principles based on belief in the sole revelation of God through Christ.

11. The Krupp family, owners of the largest ordnance works in Germany during the 19th and 20th centuries, made a fortune from the manufacture of armaments which were used in both the first and second world wars.

12. Wales has been called the Land of Song since c. 1876 when Welsh choirs began winning prizes at international music festivals. Land of the White Gloves is less well-known: it refers to the custom in Victorian times of presenting judges with white gloves when there were no cases for them to try. It derives from an idealized view of the country which held that the Welsh, in contrast to the wicked English, were a people among whom serious crime was virtually unknown.

13. Louis Blériot (1872-1936), a French aviator who made the first flight across the English Channel in 1909. The Jerry M. was a Ford lorry used by the US Army in the second world war; it was named after its designer, Jerry McCurry.

The Highest Cairn

1. This couplet is a quotation from the hymn '*Rhosymedre*', for which Morgan Rhys (1705?-70) wrote the words: '*Mae Duw yn rhoddi eto'n hael | Drugaredd i droseddwyr gwael.*'

2. 'Then came Peter to him, and said, Lord, how oft shall my brother sin against me, and I forgive him? till seven times? Jesus saith unto him, I say not unto thee, Until seven times: but Until seventy times seven.' (Matthew 18: 21, 22).

3. For Gladstone see 'The Plum Tree', note 8.

4. D. Gwenallt Jones (1899-68) was one of the greatest Welsh poets of the 20th century; the prisoner has evidently moved in literary circles. The reference to Gwenallt, author of a volume of poems entitled *Cnoi Cil* (1942), may have been suggested by the use of the verb '*cnoi cil*' (to chew it over) in the previous sentence.

5. *Yr Herald Cymraeg* ('The Welsh Herald'), a newspaper launched in 1855; *Y Cymro* ('The Welshman'), a weekly launched in 1932; for *Y Faner* see 'The Wedding', note 4.

6. 'Come now, and let us reason together, saith the Lord: though your sins be as scarlet, they shall be as white as snow; though they be red like crimson, they shall be as wool.' (Isaiah 1:18).

7. Francis of Assissi (1181-1226) was an Italian monk who founded the Order of Franciscans. His approach to religion was characterized by its joyousness and love of nature, and his rule laid great emphasis on poverty and the ascetic life.

8. William Wilberforce (1759-1833), MP for Yorkshire, devoted himself to the abolition of the slave trade and other philanthropic causes.

9. Robert Owen (1771-1858), a native of Newtown in Montgomeryshire, was a pioneer of Socialism and, from 1800, the owner of cotton mills at New Lanark, where he introduced better working conditions and generally improved the lot of workers.

10. Lewis Valentine (1893-1986), a Baptist minister and early member of Plaid Cymru. With Saunders Lewis and D. J. Williams, he was imprisoned for his part in an act of arson at the bombing range which was in the course of construction at Penyberth on the Llyn peninsula in 1936.

11. Achilles, in Greek mythology, was king of the Myrmidons. His mother dipped him in the river Styx, thus rendering him invulnerable except in the heel by which she held him. He was fatally wounded there by an arrow shot by Paris.

12. Llew Llaw Gyffes, a central character in the Fourth Branch of the Mabinogi. He can be killed only when standing with one foot on the back of a goat and the other on the edge of a tub, and under a thatched frame. Blodeuwedd, his wife, arranges for him to stand in this exact

position, whereupon her lover, Gronw Pebr, smites him with a spear. He does not die, however, but turns into an eagle, and is eventually restored to human form.

13. The Hurricane was a large aeroplane and Waltzing Matilda the nickname for a flame-throwing tank used by the Australians in the war against the Japanese; the latter was named after a song the words of which were written by Banjo Paterson (1864-1941).

14. In the Gospel according to Matthew, Jesus relates a parable about the owner of a vineyard who hires labourers at various times of the day and pays them a penny without regard to how many hours they have worked. It ends with the words: 'So the last shall be first, and the first last; for many be called, but few chosen.' (Matthew 20:16).

15. The novels *Rhys Lewis* (1885), *Gwen Tomos* (1894) and *Enoc Huws* (1891) were written by Daniel Owen (1836-95). Besides many memorable characters, they contain much moralising and discussion of theological matters.

16. Cain, according to the Book of Genesis, killed his brother Abel. Ananias, in Acts 5, together with his wife Saphira, was struck dead for lying about the price of a piece of land he had sold in order to give the proceeds to their church; his name has since become synonymous with a liar. Peter, one of the twelve apostles of Jesus, denied three times that he knew him before the cock crew, as he had been warned that he would. Judas Iscariot, another of the apostles, betrayed Jesus to the Romans by identifying him with a kiss in the Garden of Gethsemane.

17. Lewis Edwards (1809-87), essayist and theologian, founded the journal *Y Traethodydd* ('The Essayist') in 1845. Plato (c.427-c.348 BC), Greek philosopher and prose-writer, the core of whose philosophy is the doctrine of ideas: form and idea are that which remains the same through all the manifestations of a material thing or virtue. Karl Marx (1818-83), with Friedrich Engels, formulated the principles of dialectic materialism, or economic determinism, which they set out in a pamphlet, *The Communist Manifesto*, in 1848. Friedrich Nietzsche (1844-1900) was a German philosopher and poet who is best known for his theory of the Superman, which he developed in *Also sprach Zarathustra* (*Thus Spake Zarathustra*; 1883-92)

18. 'And a certain ruler asked him, saying Good Master, what shall I do to inherit eternal life? And Jesus said unto him, ... Thou knowest the commandments, Do not commit adultery, Do not kill, Do not steal, Do not bear false witness, Honour thy father and mother. And he said, All these have I kept from my youth up.' (Luke 18:21).

19. These words are a quotation from the hymn by Thomas Williams (1761-1844) of Bethesda'r Fro: '*Trugaredd wy'n ei cheisio,/ A'i cheisio eto wnaf*.

20. Snowdon (Yr Wyddfa; 3,560 ft.) is the highest mountain in Wales; the Carneddau, Lliwedd and the Aran are all mountains in north-west Wales.

The Communion

1. The name of Dyffryn Ysig, a fictitious place, may be translated as 'Valley of the Bruise'.
2. In his poem '*Nant y Mynydd*' John Ceiriog Hughes (1832-87) wrote that his heart was in the mountain with the heather and small birds: '*Mab y Mynydd ydwyf innau | Oddicartref yn gwneud cân, | Ond mae 'nghalon yn y mynydd | Efo'r grug a'r adar mân*'.
3. William Williams (1717-91) of Pantycelyn is generally considered to be one of the greatest of Welsh hymn-writers; the line "*Rwyn edrych dros y bryniau pell*' (I gaze across the distant hills) occurs in his *Gloria in Excelsis* (1772).
4. Branwen, in the Second Branch of the Mabinogi, is the wife of Matholwch, King of Ireland, who puts her to work in the kitchen of his court while the Irish and the British are at war. She sends a message to her brother, Brân, by means of a starling which she has trained to speak. Brân then invades Ireland and, in the ensuing conflict, the two islands are laid waste. On her return home, Branwen, overcome with sorrow, dies of a broken heart on the banks of the Alaw in Anglesey. Heledd, in a cycle of poems dating from the 9th or 10th century, is a member of the royal house of Powys and sister of Cynddylan, who ruled the kingdom in the early 7th century. She laments her brother's death and the destruction of his court in a verse cycle which includes the line '*Stafell Gynddylan ys tywyll heno*' ('Cynddylan's court is dark tonight').
5. We are to understand that in this story Meurig is a conscientious objector to war and military service.
6. The phrase '*Rowlio Lowri i lawr yr allt*' is a popular tongue-twister in Welsh.
7. The Pied Piper of Hamelin, in German folklore, rids the city of a plague of rats but, when the burgers refuse to pay him, he leads their children away and they vanish behind a door in the Koppenberg Hill.
8. T.S. Eliot (1888-1965) argued thus in many of his critical writings, beginning with *The Sacred Wood* in 1920.
9. Sigmund Freud (1856-1939) and his disciple Alfred Adler (1870-1937), both of whom were Austrians, were pioneers of psychoanalysis.
10. *Cymru'r Plant*, a popular children's magazine, was launched and edited by Owen M. Edwards (1858-1920); *Sioned* (1906) is a novel by Winnie

Parry (1870-1953) and *Cit* a novel by Fanny Edwards (1876-1959). The Fleece of the Yellow Sheep is a reference to a folksong, '*Croen y Dafad Felen*'.

11. Thomas Bartley is a character in the novels *Rhys Lewis* (1885) and *Enoc Huws* (1885) by Daniel Owen (1836-95). A simple, kind-hearted but crafty and sharp-witted old man, he sometimes uses English phrases such as 'to be sure'.

12. Saunders Lewis (1893-1985), playwright and critic, was jailed for his part in burning the bombing school at Penyberth in 1936. He subsequently lost his job as a Lecturer in Welsh at the University College, Swansea, and was generally ostracised. His 'disappointment' is a reference to the fact that Plaid Cymru, the party he led from 1926 to 1939, made little electoral progress during his presidency, as he himself acknowledged.

13. Morris Kyffin (c.1555-98), author and soldier, wrote a great deal of verse in both English and Welsh; his best-known poem is *The Blessedness of Brytaine* (1587) and his prose masterpiece is *Deffyniad Ffydd Eglwys Loegr* (1595), a translation of Bishop John Jewel's defence of the Anglican Church.

14. For Fellowship see 'The Wedding', note 4.

15. These words occur in several books of the New Testament, notably in the account of the Last Supper in Matthew 26:26-28: 'And as they were eating, Jesus took bread, and blessed it, and brake it, and gave it to the disciples, and said, Take, eat; this is my body. And he took the cup, and gave thanks, and gave it to them, saying, Drink ye all of it; for this is my blood of the new testament, which is shed for many for the remission of sins.' The words are are also used in Holy Communion.

On the Mend

1. Glyn and the nurse amuse each other by quoting nursery rhymes, the lines of which rhyme, as here: '*Ci a chath a chath a chi / A fi a fo a fo a fi.*'

2. The wind is known in Welsh nursery rhymes as *Morus y Gwynt*.

3. Caer Arianrhod: Arianrhod's fortress. In the Fourth Branch of the Mabinogi Arianrhod is the sister of Gwydion and mother of Llew Llawgyffes and Dylan Ail Ton.

4. Alexander the Great (356-323 BC), conqueror of the civilized world, admired for his courage and generous acts, was also a great lover of women.

5. The prose masterpiece *Gweledigaetheu y Bardd Cwsg* ('Visions of the Sleeping Bard' ; 1703) by Ellis Wynne (1671-1734) presents three

'visions' of the World, Death and Hell; the book has been translated as *The Visions of the Sleeping Bard* by George Borrow (1860), Robert Gwyneddon Davies (1897) and T. Gwynn Jones (1940).

6. This quotation is from a Welsh nursery rhyme, as is much of the dialogue in this story.

7. In the Welsh text Sali writes *ci* (dog) and Glyn reverses it by writing ic; I have avoided the inversion dog / god by substituting cat / tac.

8. The Little Black Cobbler is a character in a nursery rhyme.

9. The expression *heb siw na miw* is used to denote total silence.

10. Joseph is the child of his father's old age. His dreams evoke the jealousy of his brothers who send him into Egypt and pretend to their father that he is dead and that they have found his 'coat of many colours'. After he has risen to a position of authority in Egypt Joseph confronts his brothers and, satisfied that they have repented of their treachery, settles with them in the land of Goshen.

11. In The Book of Revelations (Chapter 6) the horses are the harbingers of the wrath of God and the end of the world.

12. This line, '*Mil harddach yw y deg ei llun*', is from the popular folksong, '*Tra Bod Dau*'.

13. This is a quotation from a poem by H. Elvet Lewis ((1860-1953), '*Rhagorfraint y Gweithiwr*': '*Nid cardod i ddyn – ond gwaith! | Mae dyn yn rhy fawr i gardod; | Mae cardod yn gadael craith, | Mae y graith yn magu nychdod.*'

The Stepping Stones

1. The name John Gwilym Jones chooses for himself in this story is taken from the account of Absalom in the second Book of Samuel in the Old Testament. Absalom, son of David, is estranged from his father after killing his half-brother Amnon in revenge for raping his sister. He rebels against his father's authority and attempts to set himself up as king in David's place. Absalom, against his father's express orders, is killed and the account ends with the king mourning his dead son: 'And the king was much moved, and went up to the chamber over the gate, and wept; and as he went, thus he said, O my son Absalom, my son, my son Absalom! Would God I had died for thee, O Absalom, my son, my son! (2 Samuel, 18:33). Tomos echoes this lamentation near the end of the story.

2. Thomas Parry (1904-85), scholar and literary critic, was a lifelong friend of the author's, as described in 'The Man from Groeslon'; Enid was his wife. For further details of their friendship see the memoir by Thomas Parry in Gwyn Thomas (ed.), *John Gwilym Jones: Cyfrol*

Deyrnged (Christopher Davies, 1974).

3. Don Pedro and Donna Theresa are characters in Donizetti's opera, *Beatrice and Benedict*, and in Shakespeare's play, *Much Ado about Nothing*.

4. *Urdd Gobaith Cymru* ('The Welsh League of Youth'), founded in 1922, holds an annual Eisteddfod at which a Chair is awarded in the poetry competition.

5. These words echo those of Mary, Christ's mother, at the wedding in Cana of Galilee, shortly before he turns water into wine: 'Whatsoever he saith unto you, do it.' (John, 2: 5)

6. The English poet William Wordsworth (1770-1850) wrote in the preface to his *Lyrical Ballads* (2nd edn., 1802), 'Poetry is the spontaneous overflow of powerful feelings: it takes its origin from emotion recollected in tranquillity.'

7. This is a quotation from *Macbeth*.

8. For the story of Branwen see 'The Communion', note 4. Gwern, the child whom Efnysien threw into the fire, was her son.

9. The Mayor of Cork who starved himself to death was Terence MacSwiney (1879-1920), writer and leader of the Cork Brigade of the Irish Republican Army. Arrested in August 1920, he began a hunger strike in Brixton Prison in an attempt to draw world attention to the Irish Republican cause; the strike lasted seventy-four days, ending with his death on 25 October.

10. The English poet Percy Bysshe Shelley (1792-1822) was drowned in the Bay of Lerici. His body was burned on the beach at Spezzia after it had been recovered by his friend Edward John Trelawney (1792-1881), who leapt into the flames to save the poet's heart.

11. Constantine is the principal character in Chekhov's play, *The Seagull*.

12. In his poem 'Ode to a Nightingale' the English poet John Keats (1795-1821) wrote, 'Darkling I listen; and, for many a time / I have been half in love with easeful Death.'

13. In the Second Branch of the Mabinogi, the gigantic Brân (or Bendigeidfran), on his way from Harlech to Ireland to avenge the wrong done to his sister Branwen, wades through the sea and lies across the river Llinon, his men using his body as a pontoon; from this episode the proverb *A fo ben bid bont* ('Let he who is a leader be a bridge') is derived.

14. Annwn is the Welsh name for the Celtic Otherworld.

15. Ynys Afallon, known in English as Avalon, was the magic island in the western ocean to which Arthur was carried after being mortally wounded in battle.

16. The wild dove is the subject of a poem, '*Y Sguthan*', by R. Williams Parry (1884-1956), in which he feels the beating of the bird's heart.

The words 'My friends going home' are from a poem by Ieuan Glan Geirionydd (Evan Evans; 1795-1855): '*Mae nghyfeillion adre'n myned / O fy mlaen o un i un.*'

17. Islwyn was the bardic name of William Thomas (1832-78), whose main work was the long poem '*Y Storm*' (1854-56). John Ceiriog Hughes (1832-87), generally known as Ceiriog, described the life and death of an Aberdyfi farmer in his poem '*Alun Mabon*'; Menna Rhen is Alun Mabon's wife.

18. The 'empty house at Rhyd Ddu' is a reference to '*Ty'r Ysgol*', a poem by T.H. Parry-Williams (1887-1975), in which he describes his home after the death of his parents.

19. In his poem '*Atgo*', Hedd Wyn (Ellis Humphrey Evans; 1887-1917) wrote (trans.), 'Only a purple moon / On the bare mountain side, / And the sound of the old river Prysor / Singing in the valley.'

Meurig

1. King John (1167-1216) was the youngest son of Henry II, against whom he rebelled, an act of treachery which broke the old king's heart. John's arbitrary practices aroused the anger of the English nobles, who compelled him to sign the Magna Carta in 1215. Dr Hawley Harvey Crippen (1861-1910) murdered his wife and buried her remains in the cellar of their London home. While trying to escape to America with his mistress, he was arrested on board ship and duly hanged.

2. The Book of Martyrs is the popular title given to John Foxe's *Actes and Monuments* (1563), a history of the Christian Church from earliest times.

3. Job is the central character in the Book of the Old Testament which bears his name. His undeserved suffering made him a by-word for patience.

4. Thomas Edward Ellis (1859-99), Liberal MP for Merioneth, was a champion of Radical causes such as Disestablishment of the Anglican Church in Wales, Home Rule and the Land Question. His apppoint-ment to the office of Junior Whip in 1892 (and Chief Whip two years later) advanced his parliamentary career at the expense of his Radical appeal in Wales. David Lloyd George (1863-1945), Liberal MP for Caernarfon, was a prominent representative of Welsh Nonconformity but after the failure of the *Cymru Fydd* movement in 1896, he virtually abandoned specifically Welsh questions and concentrated on his career as Prime Minister and world statesman. Ellis Jones-Griffith (1860-1926) was Liberal MP for Anglesey from 1895 to 1918 and for Carmarthen from 1923 to 1924.

5. The *Titanic* was a White Star liner which, during her maiden voyage, struck an iceberg in the Atlantic on 14 April 1912, sinking with the loss of more than 1,500 lives; the owners had claimed that the vessel was unsinkable.
6. For Fellowship see 'The Wedding', note 8.
7. An angel announces the birth of John the Baptist in Luke 1:13 and of Jesus in Luke 1: 31.
8. This is a reference to the nursery rhyme which begins, '*Gee, ceffyl bach yn cario ni'n dau / Dros y mynydd i hela cnau*'.
9. Pwyll, in the First Branch of the Mabinogi, is Prince of Dyfed. Arthur's knights were said to sit at a Round Table. For Branwen see 'The Communion', note 3.
10. In the Second Branch of the Mabinogi, the seven who return from the campaign in Ireland live for eighty years on the island of Gwales (Grassholm), without ageing or any remembrance of their former sorrows, until Heilyn fab Gwyn opens the closed door which faces Aber Henfelen and Cornwall; memory of the past then returns to them and they have to leave.
11. The birds of Rhiannon, in the Second Branch of the Mabinogi, are said to sing over the sea at Harlech and in the tale of Culhwch and Olwen they wake the dead and send the living to sleep.
12. These questions are taken from the Catechism.
13. *Y Drysorfa Fawr* was a magazine founded by Thomas Levi (1826-1916) and published by the Calvinistic Methodists.

Duty

1. For Menna Rhen see 'The Stepping Stones', note 17.

The Man from Groeslon

1. For Daniel Owen, see 'The Highest Cairn', note 15 and for William Williams (Pantycelyn), see 'The Communion', note 3.
2. Aristotle (384-322 BC) was a Greek philosopher whose *Poetics* is his main contribution to literary criticism.
3. Ida Haendel (b.1924), Polish violinist; Anais Nin (1914-78), American novelist.
4. 'Gerontion'(1920), a poem by T. S. Eliot (1888-1965), is spoken by 'an old man in a dry month'; it is full of despair about old age, aridity, the spiritual decay of the world, and the need and unlikelihood of salvation.

5. For Fellowship see 'The Wedding', note 8.

6. Wil Bryan and Rhys Lewis are characters in the plays *Rhys Lewis* (1885) and *Enoc Huws* (1891) by Daniel Owen 1836-95); see also 'The Highest Cairn', note 15 and 'The Communion', note 11.

7. Saunders Lewis (1893-1985) was the grandson of Dr Owen Thomas (1812-91), author of a celebrated biography of John Jones (1796-1857) of Tal-y-sarn.

8. Cilla Black (the stage-name of Priscilla White; b.1943), singer and host of TV game-shows, including *Blind Date*, was born in Liverpool and speaks with a strong Liverpudlian accent.

9. For Lord Newborough and Glynllifon see note 19 below.

10. Malvolio, a character in Shakespeare's *Twelfth Night* (1601), is a smug, pompous fool who secretly aspires to his employer's love. He says, 'But be not afraid of greatness: some men are born great, some achieve greatness, and some have greatness thrust upon them.' (Act 2, scene 5).

11. R.G. Collingwood (1889-1943), English philosopher and archaeologist.

12. Martin Luther (1483-1546) was a German religious reformer whose critique of the Catholic Church was the beginning of the Protestant Reformation. John Bunyan (1628-88), author of *The Pilgrim's Progress* (1678, 1684). For William Wilberforce see 'The Highest Cairn', note 8. Charles Stewart Parnell (1846-91), Irish Nationalist leader who championed the cause of Home Rule. Emmeline Pankhurst (1858-1928), English suffragette. The Daughters of Rebecca were bands of men disguised as women who attacked toll-gates in south-west Wales in the mid-19th century. Jac Glan-y-gors was the sobriquet of John Jones (1766-1821), a satirical poet. John Penry (1563-93), Welsh Puritan pamphleteer, was executed for having written tracts against the corruption of the bishops of the Church of England.

13. Robespierre was responsible for the Terror which followed the French Revolution of 1789. Nikolai Alexsandrovitch Berdyaev (1874-1948), philosopher who played a leading part in the renaissance of religious thought in Russia in the early 20th century.

14. W. B. Yeats (1865-1939) wrote his poem 'The Lake Isle of Innisfree' in 1893. After the Easter Rising of 1916, during which Patrick Pearse and others proclaimed the Irish Republic and were executed for it, he wrote some of his best patriotic poems, including 'Easter, 1916' in 1921. The lines beginning 'You that Mitchel's prayer have heard' are from the poem 'Under Ben Bulben' (1938). John Mitchel (1815-75) was an Irish journalist and revolutionary who founded the newspaper, *The United Irishman*, in 1847.

15. R. Williams Parry (1884-1956) wrote some of his most acerbic poems after the burning of the RAF bombing-school at Penyberth on the Llyn peninsula, for which Saunders Lewis and his co-arsonists were gaoled.

The words '*Cymer fyny dy wely a rhodia, O Wynt*' are the first line of his poem '*Cymru 1937*', in which he chastises the Welsh people for their indifference.

16. Ieuan Gwyllt was the bardic name of John Roberts (1822-77), musician and editor, who did much to spread a knowledge of tonic sol-fa among the people of Wales.

17. *Cymru'r Plant* and *Cymru Coch* were magazines launched and edited by Owen M. Edwards (1858-1920).

18. The Red Bandits of Mawddwy (*Gwylliaid Cochion Mawddwy*) were a band of outlaws who lived in Merioneth in the 16th century.

19. F.G. Wynne was the great-grandson of the first Lord Newborough, but did not inherit the title. Glynllifon and the Belan fort on the Menai Straits belonged to his father; the house was subsequently bought by Gwynedd County Council and used as a College of Agriculture. Wynne's great-grandmother, Maria Stella Petronilla Chiappini (1773-1843), wrote her memoirs (1830) in which she claimed to be the heiress to the throne of France, having been substituted for the male child of a poor Italian family by her real father, the Comte de Joinville (1747-93), the Duke of Orleans, a member of the French royal family. The claim was not grounded in fact and there is no reference to it on the memorial to Lady Newborough in the church at Llandwrog. For further details see Bruce Griffiths, '*Yr Ymhonwyr*', in Dafydd Glyn Jones and John Ellis Jones (eds.), *Bosworth a'r Tuduriaid* (1985).

20. Kate Roberts (1891-1985), novelist and short-story writer, a native of Rhosgadfan, not far from Groeslon, is generally considered to be the greatest Welsh short-story writer of the 20th century.

21. *The Pilgrim's Progress* (1678, 1684), a prose allegory of the Christian life, was the most celebrated work of John Bunyan (1628-88).

22. William Rathbone (1819-1902) was Liberal MP for Caernarfonshire from 1880 to 1885 and for the Arfon Division of Caernarfon from 1885 to 1895.

23. Shân Emlyn (1936-99), musician and folksong adjudicator, was the first wife of Owen Edwards, the former Controller of S4C.

24. John Gwilym Jones won the Prose Medal at the National Eisteddfod held at Denbigh in 1939 with his short novel, *Y Dewis*, and the Drama Competition with his play *Diofal yw Dim*.

25. For Thomas Parry see 'The Stepping Stones', note 2.

26. The story of Eli and the child Samuel, on whom God called, is told in the third chapter of the first Book of Samuel.

27. Elen Luyddawg, known in English as Helen of the Hosts, is the heroine of *The Dream of Macsen Wledig*, one of the two historical tales included in *The Mabinogion*. Many roads in Wales are known as Sarn Helen.

28. Hernando Cortès or Cortez (1485-1547) was the Spanish conqueror

of Mexico.

29. The Disestablishment of the Anglican Church in Wales was an issue which caused bitter political and religious controversy during the second half of the 19th century and the first two decades of the 20th. The Church was disestablished by Lloyd George's Liberal administration in 1920 and was known thereafter as the Church in Wales.

30. Plaid Cymru, now also known as the Party of Wales, was founded in 1925.

31. For Lloyd George see 'Meurig', note 4 ; for Lewis Valentine see 'The Highest Cairn', note 10.

32. Robin Lewis (b. 1929) was the Plaid Cymru candidate in Caernarfonshire at the General Election of 1970; he came second, receiving 11,331 votes against the sitting candidate, Goronwy Roberts, who polled 13,627; he is currently Archdruid of Wales.

33. This line is from the second stanza of the poem 'Morality' by Matthew Arnold (1822-88).

34. *Llais Llyfrau* (*Book News*) was a trade journal published by the Welsh Books Council. T. Wilson Evans (b.1928) is a Welsh novelist.

35. *Cwrs y Byd* ('The World's Course') is part of Ellis Wynne's prose masterpiece *Gweledigaetheu y Bardd Cwsc* (1703).

36. A Wrangler is a graduate of Cambridge University who has obtained first-class honours in the Mathematics Tripos.

37. Ivanhoe is the eponymous hero of a novel by Sir Walter Scott (1771-1832). The Lady of the Lake, in Malory's *Morte d'Arthur* (c.1469) and Tennyson's *Idylls of the King* (1859-85), lives in a castle in the middle of a magical lake; it is from her that Arthur receives the sword Excalibur. Macbeth, in Shakespeare's play of the same name (c. 1606), is prophetically hailed by three witches as Thane of Glamis, Thane of Cawdor and future king of Scotland.

38. For *Y Bardd Cwsg* (The Sleeping Bard) see 'On the Mend', note 4. *Môr y Canoldir a'r Aifft* (1913) was written by T. Gwynn Jones (1871-1949) in the Mediterranean and Egypt, where he had gone to recover his health. '*Cywydd y Farn Fawr*' ('Cywydd of the Great Judgement'), a poem by Goronwy Owen (1723-69), was written in 1752. *Telynegion Maes a Môr* is a volume of lyrics by Eifion Wyn (Eliseus Williams; 1867-1926).

39. Leila Megane (Margaret Jones; 1891-1960) was the most popular singer in Wales in the 1920s and 1930s.

40. Ifor Williams (1881-1965) was Professor of Welsh at the University College of North Wales from 1920 to 1947.

41. Tair G, the name by which *Y Gymdeithas Genedlaethol Gymreig* was known, a society of Nationalists at the University College of North Wales who joined other groups to form Plaid Cymru in 1925.

42. *Y Ddraenen Wen* (1922) is a play by R.G. Berry (1869-1945) and *Gwyntoedd Croesion* (translated as *Cross Currents*, 1923) a play by J.O. Francis (1882-1956).

43. *A Doll's House* (*Et Dukkehjem*,1879) is one of the most powerful plays of Henrik Ibsen (1828-1906) in which Nora is the tragic heroine.

44. Richard Lawrence Archer ('Daddy Archer'; 1874-1953) was Professor of Education at the University College of North Wales, Bangor, from 1906 to 1942.

45. John Edward Jones (1905-70) was Secretary of Plaid Cymru from 1930 to 1962. O.M. Roberts (1906-99) was a prominent member of Plaid Cymru and one of those who helped to carry out an act of arson at Penyberth in the Llyn peninsula in 1936.

46. Box Hill, in Surrey, was a favourite recreational haunt for Londoners. Arsenal is a football club founded in 1884 by workers at the Royal Arsenal in Woolwich. Wimbledon is the home of international tennis.

47. Fritz Kreisler (1875-1962) was an Austrian violin virtuoso and composer. Johann Sebastian Bach (1685-1750) composed Chaconne (or Passacaglia), a form of music which had its origins in Spanish dance.

48. The Proms are a series of promenade concerts which have been held in London since 1838; Henry Wood (1869-1944) became their principal conductor in 1895.

49. Sir Thomas Beecham(1879-1961), English conductor noted for the performance of works by Mozart, Delius and Handel, including *The Messiah*.

50. Sir Emrys Evans (1891-1966), classical scholar, was Principal of the University College of North Wales, Bangor, from 1927 to1958.

51. The poet T. Gwynn Jones (1871-1949) became Professor of Welsh at University College, Aberystwyth, in 1919, despite his lack of academic qualifications.

Acknowledgements

The publisher is grateful for the permission of the literary estate of John Gwilym Jones, and in particular for the kind co-operation of Mr Arthur Wyn Parry of Groeslon.

The permission of Gwasg Gee, publisher of *Y Goeden Eirin* (1946), and of Ty ar y Graig, publisher of the autobiographical radio-talk by John Gwilym Jones which appeared in the volume *Atgofion* (vol.1, 1972), is also acknowledged.

The translator wishes to thank the following for their assistance: Professor Emeritus Gwyn Thomas and Mr Don Dale-Jones for reading a near-final draft of the text; the Reverend Cynwil Williams for help with theological matters; Professor Elan Closs Stephens, Mr Dafydd Glyn Jones and Dr Bruce Griffiths for elucidating a number of local references; Professor Emeritus Hywel Teifi Edwards, Dr Sandra Anstey and Mr Alan Llwyd for helping to identify some of the literary allusions; and Mr Tony Burke, Librarian of Welsh National Opera, for help with Don Pedro and Donna Theresa.